A Matter of Time

A Matter of Time

Sheri Cooper Sinykin

MARSHALL CAVENDISH   NEW YORK

Marshall Cavendish Corporation
99 White Plains Road
Tarrytown, New York 10591

Library of Congress Cataloging-in-Publication Data
Sinykin, Sheri Cooper
A matter of time/Sheri Cooper Sinykin,
p. cm.
Summary: When Jody, a sixth grade boy, travels back in time to when his
father was his age, he is finally able to mend their fragile relationship.
ISBN 0-7614-5019-X
[1. Time travel—Fiction. 2. Fathers and sons—Fiction.
3. Grandmothers—Fiction.] I. Title.
PZ7.S6194Mat [Fic]—dc21 97-3433 CIP AC

The text of this book is set in 12 point Meridien
Book design by Constance Ftera
Printed in the United States of America

With thanks, especially to Stephanie G. Lowden,
Patricia Curtis Pfitsch, Suzanne Jennings, Catherine Frey
Murphy, K. Skogen-Johnson, Marilyn E. Marlow, and
Judith R. Whipple.

Finally, for Daniel—
my travelmate in time
who enables all my greatest joys.

Chapter 1

◉ Amazing. It was almost seven o'clock, the night before Easter, and Scott had actually jumped at Jody's invitation to come right over. But now, as Jody rummaged through his closet and scanned his messy bedroom, worry worked his stomach into knots. Once Scott gets here, *then* what?

Playing with plastic building bricks and board games was definitely not cool anymore. Not for sixth graders. Scott was into sports-card collecting, Jody knew—not that he himself had any good ones to trade or brag about. Grandma Anderson, unfortunately, had seen to that by throwing away Dad's Mickey Mantle, among others. At least there were always video games—and TV, of course. With all those cable channels, something good *had* to be on. Where was the weekly program guide? Maybe his parents had seen it.

With Mugsy tagging along in a tinkle of bells, Jody headed toward their bedroom. "I hope Scott's not allergic to you, Mugs," he said to the fat, smoke-gray calico. The last kid he'd gotten up the nerve to invite over had practically broken out in hives the minute he took his coat off. At the memory, Jody's cheeks went hot all over again. So much for *that* almost-best friendship.

At the end of the hall, Mugsy nudged the door open and slipped into the master bedroom. Jody hesitated, unsure whether to knock or to simply walk in.

"Tom? What is it?" Mom's concerned tone riveted Jody in place. "What did he say?"

Through the narrow opening, Jody saw his father slowly shake his head and tug at his beard. "It's just a matter of time, Ellen. He says there's nothing I can do right now."

"No one else you can talk to? It's really that hopeless? Are you sure?"

Somehow Dad's sigh kept Jody from even blinking. "Looks that way, hon."

His parents hugged then, walling Jody out. Alone in the unlit hallway, he struggled to piece together an explanation. He had to stay calm. Not overreact. But his mind would not obey. In an instant, it was replaying scenes from a TV movie of the week. What if his parents were being superprotective like the ones in *Six Months to Live*? Those guys never even told their kid that her father was dying.

No, Jody thought. That couldn't be it. Dad looked fine. Lost a few pounds, maybe. But that was on purpose, wasn't it? Still, hadn't he said something about having an important appointment last week? What if it was with the doctor? What if Dad's test results came back "hopeless, just a matter of time"?

Jody's chest felt near to bursting, and he realized

he'd forgotten to breathe. All he got for his effort, though, was a strange hiccupy sound that made his parents turn in surprise toward the doorway. Dad *couldn't* be dying. Jody was probably just jumping to conclusions. Again.

Frozen in the awkward silence, Jody braced himself. For what? he wondered. The truth, or a lecture about eavesdropping?

"Did you want something?" his mother asked.

I want Dad to be okay. But the words seemed to stick in the back of his throat. He blinked at his mother, saw her lips move again, but somehow couldn't hear her. It was as if someone had hit her mute button.

Dad snapped his fingers only inches from Jody's face. "Hey, Joe, snap out of it. What's wrong, huh?"

"Wrong? *Wrong?*" His voice climbed dangerously.

"It just seemed like you wanted something, that's all," Dad said.

"Wanted, um . . . yes." Jody swam backward in his mind, away from the sucking black hole of Dad's imagined death. "What I wanted . . . right . . . was the TV listings." He blinked up at his father and saw only a blur, a cardboard father-person. Nothing more. You can't die, his mind screamed. Not yet. I don't even *know* you. Not really. Not the way I know Mom. . . .

Dad's tone of voice was so soothingly everything's-back-to-normal-now that it took a moment for Jody to tune in to what he was saying. "Television again! I thought you were going to cut back on that and start

11

asking the Livesey boy over. Honestly, Jody, when I was your age, we used to—"

"I *did* ask," Jody cut in. "And he *is* coming, okay? I was just . . ." His voice trailed off. There was no way he was going to get into this same old discussion about Dad's perfect childhood without television. Especially now, with him standing there, putting on a brave front for Jody's sake. Maybe under that dark beard of his, he was hiding deadly moles, chock full of skin cancer. Or what if a rare tropical brain fog was draining the life right out of him, just like it had done to Terry on *All My Days*?

"Jody?" Mom frowned, and Jody avoided her eyes. They were like radar, able to home in on any blip that might threaten his happiness. "What is it, hon?"

How could she even ask! Jody gaped at her, understanding slow in coming. Sure, that *had* to be the reason. She was caught. What could she say in front of Dad? It would be just like him not to want anyone else to know. Better to ask her later, when she and Jody were alone. "It's . . . nothing," he said. "We can . . . it can wait."

Dad seemed to wince at Jody's words, and Jody realized that he'd seen that look many times before. He had never understood it, though. Never considered that Dad might have been in pain.

As if through a blanket of sleep, Jody heard the doorbell chiming faintly from downstairs. "That's Scott! I'll get it!" He hated how loud and phony he sounded.

"Could be the Brauns," Mom called after him. "Tell

them we'll be right down. And put the bridge mix out, will you, honey?"

"The *what*?"

"The candy dish. The one with the nuts and raisins and chocolate chips."

Like a shadow, Mugsy appeared at Jody's feet, nearly tripping him on the way downstairs. When Jody's digital watch beeped, marking the hour, the cat blinked up at him with scolding gold eyes.

"I know, I know," Jody said, remembering he was supposed to switch to Daylight Savings Time tonight. "Spring forward. But first I've got to find the instructions."

Thanks to the porch light, he could see Scott framed in the foyer window. Though the big blond kid made Jody feel short by comparison, Scott was quick to smile, slow to complain, and lived right around the corner. He hadn't grown up in the Midwest either—all of which made him possible best friend material. Jody waved, then opened the door. "Hi. Come on in, only don't let the cat out, okay?"

Scott scooped Mugsy up and set her down again inside. He wasn't wearing a jacket, and his bare arms bristled from the early April chill. Rubbing his reddened skin, Scott laughed. "Weatherman said warming, but I guess he didn't mean right now."

"Yeah." Jody nodded. "Tomorrow, maybe."

"Yeah, tomorrow." Scott stuffed his hands into his pockets and kind of nodded back as if they'd both said something significant.

"I'm sick of winter, aren't you? I still can't believe how long it hangs on around here. Not like in San Diego, that's for sure."

"Not like in Phoenix, either." Scott sighed.

Jody, suddenly squirmy in the silence, searched for something else, something better—maybe even funny—to say. He needed to take his mind off what he'd overheard upstairs.

"Uh, I can't stay long. An hour, Mom said. We're getting up early to go to my grandma's, down near Chicago. And I still have to pack."

"Sure." Jody supposed he could have told Scott that his own grandmother lived in town, that they planned to have Easter dinner with her at the nursing home. But Grandma Anderson was like air to him, there but not really, and he didn't like to talk about her. "So, what do you want to do?"

Scott shrugged. "It's your house."

Jody hated this moment, this decision. And yet ever since they'd moved to Wisconsin, it always seemed to come. As predictable, he thought, as the local TV commercial at twenty-eight minutes after the hour and two minutes before. He dreaded having to guess which of his suggestions might be met with enthusiasm rather than indifference or, worse yet, scorn. Why couldn't making friends here be no big deal like it was in San Diego? "You want to see my room?"

"Sure."

Jody led the way upstairs, then, remembering the

snack mix, excused himself for a minute to go sneak a few handfuls for himself and Scott. He glanced about the just-tidied family room, where his parents had added a folding table and chairs and a fresh deck of cards. Play bridge. That's what grown-ups did for fun with *their* friends. Somehow it seemed like a boring waste of time. Mugsy streaked past then—bent on mischief, Jody could tell—and bounded onto Dad's leather chair, the only place in the house that was truly off-limits to them both.

"Get off there, Mugs," he scolded.

But the cat only smiled as if she had a secret.

Jody whisked her up and immediately noticed the program guide wedged between the cushion and the armrest. Grinning at Mugsy, he gave her cross-eyed nose-kisses until at last the old cat purred. Then he turned to the Saturday section to search for something so scary that he'd forget for a while about what he'd overheard—and what it all meant. No doubt he'd find out the truth once he had a chance to talk to Mom.

Jody scanned the lineup. Game shows, a western, Nick at Nite, a movie he'd seen before on HBO. Nothing seemed quite right. He blew out a long breath. What was the point of having thirty-six channels if they were all as boring as bridge?

Jody had to hurry. Scott would be wondering where he was. Flipping the page, he noticed a promo for a new sci-fi channel. A freebie on Cable Four all weekend.

"Hey, Mugs," Jody whispered, "listen to this. *War of*

the Graveyard Ghouls." Just saying the title of the seven o'clock movie raised icy-fingered goose bumps on the back of his neck. Perfect! With one zap of the remote, Jody realized, he could make all his worries disappear— at least for the next two hours.

Chapter 2

With his parents and their friends downstairs, already debating how best to bid their bridge hands, Jody claimed the master bedroom TV for himself and Scott. "This movie sounds awesome," Jody said, plumping one of the beanbag chairs he'd dragged in from his own room. "You like scary stuff, don't you?"

"Who doesn't?"

Jody lowered the volume guiltily—no sense advertising to his parents through the heat vent that he was watching TV again—then closed their door.

"It's okay if we're in here, right?" Scott asked.

"Oh, sure." As convincingly as he could, Jody tried to wave away his friend's concern. "I do it all the time." Which was at least accurate if not the whole truth. Actually, he wasn't sure *how* his parents would feel about Scott being in there. But he *was* company, after all, and if he wanted to watch TV, where else were they going to go? Jody settled back, crunching the beans around beneath him until he was comfortable.

"What *is* a graveyard ghoul, anyway?"

"A grave robber, I think," Jody said. "Can you hear okay?" Though Scott only shrugged, Jody inched the volume higher. On the television screen, gray tomb-stones pierced an eerie fog. As the camera zoomed in on a chiseled name above a freshly dug grave, Jody strained to read it. Thomas A-something.

Instantly, he imagined *Thomas Anderson*, his father's name, on the granite marker, and his pulse quickened. But no. It was definitely something shorter than Anderson. Andrews, maybe.

"What's with you?" Scott eyed him strangely.

Jody steadied his breathing, eased his tense forehead back into neutral. Maybe if he knew Scott better, he'd tell him what was really on his mind. But there was no way he was going to talk about something creepy like death with a total stranger, almost. Even if Scott *was* his could-be best friend.

"I'm just getting into this, that's all," Jody replied at last, hoping it was true, that the color images on the TV screen would swirl him up and away . . . and soon.

At the sound of someone on the stairs, Jody startled awake and punched the power-off button on the remote. He vaguely remembered having said good-bye to Scott—an absent wave, a mechanical "See ya, thanks for coming over." But that was right at a good part, and Jody had no idea how Scott had made himself leave in the middle of it. Now, from the looks of that infomercial on Cable Four, it was late, way past his parents' usual ten-thirty bedtime.

As he untangled himself from the bedspread nest he'd made on the floor between the beanbag chairs, his mother appeared in the doorway. "What're you still doing up?" she whispered, as if there were someone nearby she didn't want to awaken. "Scott left hours ago."

Jody nodded and tried to stifle a yawn. "I wanted to talk to you," he said. "It's about Dad. Where is . . . ? He's okay, isn't he?" Did his mother hear the panic in his voice, too?

"Of course he's okay." Mom brushed her hand affectionately over his spikey haircut and smiled. "He's just playing around with a new idea for his column. He'll be up in a minute."

Jody's lips twitched to one side. He knew how long his father's minutes were—more like hours, once he sat down at his computer. It was always the same old apology, the same old excuse. Somehow with Dad, "playing around" usually ended up meaning "working overtime." Jody wondered whether, to his father, there was even a difference.

Mom picked up the bedspread, offering Jody the other end so he could help fold it. "You said you wanted to talk," she prompted him.

"I do, only . . . You promise you'll tell me the truth?"

"Have you ever known me to lie?"

"Not on purpose," Jody said. "Not unless you have a good reason to."

His mother patted the edge of the bed, and Jody sat beside her. Suddenly, he felt like a little kid on the verge of letting his cleaned-up room loose from an overstuffed closet. Maybe it was safer not to even open the door. . . . "You're *sure* Dad's all right?" he asked at last.

"Positive. But if you'd like to see for yourself, I could—"

"I mean, he's not dying or anything?"

"Dying? Why on earth . . . ? Of course, he's not dying, Jody." Mom cupped his chin in her hand and looked him squarely in the eyes. "What would make you think a thing like that?"

Jody studied her expression for any hint of evasion, but found none. "Something he said before, when he was on the phone." When his mother only frowned, Jody pressed on, quoting what he'd overheard as accurately as if he were a tape recorder.

"Oh, honey." Mom hugged him close. "You've got it all wrong. Your dad didn't get the promotion he's been hoping for, that's all."

Jody wanted to believe her. He really did. But what kind of a person would call with such news on a Saturday night—let alone on the one before Easter? It was a good try, but he knew how protective mothers were of their kids. Even in that movie he'd just watched, after the lady finally escaped the graveyard ghouls, she wouldn't even tell her son. It's for his own good, she had said. Though that wasn't actually how things had turned out in the end. . . . Jody tried not to think about it, tried to believe that *his* mother really was telling the truth. But why, then, couldn't he feel relieved or stupid or *something* besides scared? "I guess I shouldn't have been listening," he said at last.

Mom nodded. "It's easy to jump to the wrong conclusion, isn't it?"

"I guess." Still, he wondered, wasn't it just as easy to jump to the *right* one?

"So, did you and Scott have fun? What'd you do?"

Jody shrugged. "You know. Just talked and stuff."

"He seems like a nice boy. Reminds me a little of—"

"Yeah, I know," Jody said, certain she was thinking of his best growing-up friend in San Diego, the one who hadn't written or called as he'd promised—but then, neither had Jody. Now it seemed more like ten years than two since the move to Dad's hometown. A whole other lifetime, practically.

"You look tired," Mom said. "I'll walk you down the hall."

"And tuck me in?"

"Quickly. Before your father comes up."

Jody gave her a hug and a thin smile of gratitude. Unlike Dad, she, at least, seemed to understand that sometimes he still needed to feel like a little kid.

On the way to Jody's room, the nightlight in the hall threw their shadows, long and gaunt, before them. Noting their ghoulish resemblance, Jody shuddered.

"You cold?" Mom slipped her arm around his shoulder and rubbed it for a moment.

Jody considered admitting that he'd watched that dumb old graveyard movie. But what was the point? He knew exactly what she'd say—that he wasn't supposed to, that now his imagination was only going to run away with itself, and hadn't they been through all this before? "I guess I am a little cold," Jody said instead, and tucked the warmth and safety of her touch away for later, in the middle of the night, when he knew he would need it. "That helps a lot."

When Jody came down for breakfast the next morning, his father was standing over a sizzling griddle, turning pieces of French toast. Steam, rich with cinnamon and vanilla, hovered beneath the hood fan that Mom would have been quick to turn on. "Hey, Joe, what do you know?" Dad greeted him. "Happy Easter!"

"Yeah, Happy Easter." Jody hoped he didn't sound as glum as he felt. But, really, the way they celebrated Easter made it seem more like the Halloween of Spring, with too-small church clothes for costumes, and plastic grass—not pumpkins—for holding all his treats.

"Grab me another stick of butter, would you?" Dad asked.

Though the flat pan was already slick with shortening, Jody handed him a hard new cube, then watched his father carve off more chunks and slip them beneath the bright yellow bread squares. Maybe using a lot of butter was the secret to making Dad's famous French toast. That, melted with more than a little powdered sugar on top. At the thought, Jody felt somehow disappointed. What if, the hint of mystery gone, Dad's special breakfast never again tasted quite so good?

"Hope you're hungry, Joe. I'm making enough for an army, looks like."

"Where's Mom?"

"Sleeping in. Guess I talked her ear off last night. You know how I get when I'm working on something new. Wired."

Jody nodded, noticing his father had said he'd been *working*, not *playing*—just as Jody had suspected. He doubted that Dad even knew how to play anymore, if he ever had in the first place.

"I'll probably crash this afternoon, though." Dad handed him a plate and rushed on as if he'd already drunk a whole pot of coffee. "Three slices or four? Start with three, okay? There's plenty. I just love it when all the pieces come together in my mind, like a puzzle—you know?—but then the real trick is turning that picture into words."

Jody poked through the traditional candy-and-plastic-grass-filled basket that had been left for him on the counter. "We're still going to Grandma's, aren't we?"

"It's Sunday, isn't it? No complaints. I want to see some Easter spirit around here."

"Who's complaining? I was just asking, that's all. You

said you were probably going to take a nap, and I thought—"

"If I do, then you and your mom can bike over without me, and I'll meet you there for supper."

"But . . . are you sure you're okay?" Jody blurted to his own surprise. He guessed that talk with his mother last night hadn't put an end to his doubts after all. "Maybe you shouldn't be here alone."

"Hey, I'm a big boy," Dad teased, joining Jody at the kitchen table. "I think I can handle it."

"Not if you're really sick or something." Jody studied his father's reaction, but could read nothing beyond his frown. "I mean, what if you were . . . dying?" Somehow the word managed to slip past the knot in Jody's throat. "You're not, are you?"

Dad's laugh sounded forced and unnatural. "Well, we're *all* dying, Jody. Hopefully, just not today." Dad reached for the Sunday paper.

"I . . . uh . . ." Jody gaped slack-jawed as his father calmly blotted his lips and brushed powdered sugar from his beard with a paper napkin. "I guess I never thought about it like that before," he said at last.

"A shame, isn't it?" Dad nodded sympathetically. "Few people do. Not until it's too late." He opened the family section then, no doubt looking for his column.

The finality of the way he said *late* rang in Jody's ears until, little by little, only the echo of his fear remained. So what if he'd jumped to conclusions and imagined the worst? What difference did *that* make? Jody's racing pulse and watery eyes had felt real. *Were* real, he decided. As real as if Dad *had* gotten bad news from the doctor. "I don't want it to ever be too late, Dad," Jody said, as soft as praying.

But his father, hunched over the newspaper, appeared not to hear.

Chapter 3

◎ Instead of taking a nap, Dad ended up working on his column. "Just a couple more sentences, Ellen," he kept saying all afternoon, and then at last, "Why don't you and Jody go on? I'll catch up with you there."

Maybe it's just as well, Jody thought as he and Mom headed out on their bicycles. Who knows? Grandma might be having a *good* day for a change, the kind the nurses sometimes talked about but that he himself had never seen. It would be so cool if she could remember and actually tell him some "when-your-father-was-your-age" stories. . . .

"You look awfully eager to get there," Mom commented.

"Yeah, I guess I am." Jody heard the surprise in his voice. Block by block, however, his enthusiasm seemed to leak away like air from an old balloon. Then, suddenly, he knew why, and a strange sense of foreboding rushed in to make his chest go tight.

Ahead on his right, the cemetery near Sunnyview

Home loomed like a stark gray city. As he drew nearer, bare branches chittering in the wind called up images of dancing skeletons from last night's movie. He knew the graveyard would stretch on until the nursing home, and he shuddered, imagining ghouls lying in wait for him somewhere along the way.

"Stop it, Jody," he said, forcing himself to look closer. "Get a grip." He could see that since last week's spring thaw, the grounds were paved now with mud and brittle grass. Paperwhites and crocuses peeked among the headstones. Splashes of living color among the dead. Jody laughed hollowly. Too much TV on the brain. Definitely.

Realizing with a start that his mother had pulled ahead, he leaned harder on his pedals. It wasn't that she was speeding—just that *he* had to make do with a stupid old clunker. If only his dirt bike hadn't been stolen, he'd have been able to keep up with her. No sweat. He supposed he should be grateful he had *any* wheels to ride, but the jokes about his Tyrannosaurus Wreck were getting old. He'd never understand why, after selling Grandma's house and moving her into Sunnyview, Dad had insisted on keeping such a rusty bike (not to mention a whole mess of other junk) in their new basement. As if anybody would ever want that stuff. "Hey, Mom! Wait up!"

As she circled back, Jody sneaked another glance at the cemetery and kept pumping. Grandpa Anderson was buried there, along with who-knew-how-many recent residents of the nursing home. Had any of them stared out at him last week through vacant eyes or extended bony fingers his way when he'd passed their wheelchairs? Jody shivered at the creepy thought, half-expecting an aura, an energy, to come rising from some dark mound of earth, calling him to a freshly dug grave.

"I *don't* believe in spooks, I *don't* believe in spooks," he whispered over and over again, adapting a line from his beloved movie, *The Wizard of Oz*. He should have watched that movie last night. Mom and Dad wouldn't have minded, would they?

"I'm too fast for you, huh?" Mom teased.

"Not for *me*," Jody said, "for this bike. What do you want to bet the chain falls off!"

"Come on. We're almost there."

"Do you think . . . ?" Jody licked his lips, pressed on. "Can we go the back way, down past the park?"

"But that takes longer and I thought you were—"

"The cemetery's giving me the creeps today, okay?" There. He'd admitted it. He supposed he'd better brace himself for a mess of questions. Would she argue? Say, "No way. We're late already"? Make fun of him for being scared? Dad might have, but Mom simply shrugged. As they crossed the street and headed toward the wooden jungle-climber, Jody turned to her and smiled. "Thanks."

She didn't even ask, "For what?" It was as if she'd already read his mind. Jody wished she could teach him how to do that. He'd try it on Dad and on Grandma, too. Just knowing *any* of her thoughts would make his visits a lot less frustrating.

At the nursing home, Mom went into Grandma's room alone to make sure she was up and dressed. Jody waited outside in the hallway, hoping that somehow today things would be different. Usually his grandmother would be sitting in her straight-backed rocker, her hair, long and silvery-brown, spilling like pulled taffy over one shoulder. Always before, she'd be stroking it absently and staring out the window. But today—maybe finally today—she'd turn and look at him and know who he was. Then she'd smile and invite him to sit on her lap (though being too big for it, he would decline, of course) and launch into a story about what Little Tommy Anderson did back in the olden days, when Dad used to be perfect. . . .

"She's not quite ready for us, hon." Mom tiptoed out and closed the door. "But by the time Dad gets here—"

"Where should we wait, then? In the TV room?" Maybe the Jeopardy Gang would be there. Jody didn't mind going up against the few residents who were still on top of things. It helped take his mind off the ones like Grandma who usually weren't.

"Oh, no you don't. Aren't you supposed to be starting a TV diet?" Mom plucked him back by the T-shirt. Jody sighed and said nothing. "Besides," she added, "he'll be here any minute."

Actually, it took more like *sixteen* minutes and forty-three seconds, according to the CHRONO mode on Jody's watch. He supposed it could have been worse, though, considering how long most of his father's "minutes" turned out to be.

"Mama?" Dad knocked on his mother's door, then nudged it open.

Grandma turned, regarding them blankly.

"It's Tom, Mama. And Ellen and Jody."

"Ellen and Jody?" Grandma's hands appeared to wash themselves of stale air.

"Joseph Douglas, your grandson," Dad said. "And you know Ellen, Mama."

Mom and Dad advanced into the room then, but Jody hung back. Why had he thought today's visit would be any different from all the others? He must be as crazy as his grandmother was, getting his hopes up like that.

"Come on, Jody," Dad urged. "Come give Grandma a kiss now."

She'd better not pinch me like last time, he thought, turning on a smile and inching forward. His gaze took in the familiar framed pictures on her dresser, the crocheted runner on which they rested. According to Dad, Grandma herself had made that. Still, Jody couldn't quite imagine those fingers, knobbled now with arthritis, producing anything so complicated and fine.

"Hi, Grandma," he said, forcing a brightness he wished he could feel. He bent toward her, and though her skin reeked of some kind of ointment, he made his lips brush her wrinkled cheek.

"Billy?" Grandma looked from Jody to Dad. "You brought Billy to see me?"

"Bill's in Florida, Ma, remember? He lives down there now."

Jody supposed he should be grateful that Grandma Anderson never thought he was Aunt Sally, who lived far away, too. He himself scarcely knew Dad's older sister *or* Uncle Billy. But from the snapshots on Grandma's wall, he'd at least recognize them if they were to ever show up out of nowhere.

"You're sure you're not Billy?"

"Very sure, Grandma."

"Wasn't he here a few minutes ago? Yes, I'm sure he was. And now you've scared him into hiding." Grandma hugged herself and began rocking in an agitated sort of way.

Mom rushed over, all coos and reassurances. Dad offered Grandma sips of cranberry juice from a glass on her nightstand.

Jody checked his watch and sighed, then remembered that he still hadn't set it ahead. Unlike the two-hand style that his parents had insisted he learn to tell time on, this face was digital and easy to read. It also glowed in the dark, which just about made up for what a pain it was to reset. Mentally, he added an hour to 3:47— making it 4:47. Still, what were they all going to do until dinner at five-thirty?

After several attempts at conversation with Grandma, Mom whispered, "Jody, why don't you go get a wheel-chair? We'll take her for a little ride until supper, okay?"

He nodded, relieved to have an errand. Maybe it was

31

this place that made Grandma act strangely. Why would anyone build a nursing home so close to a cemetery? Restless spirits were probably calling out to their old neighbors all the time. No wonder Grandma and the others were so confused and sat around gabbling nonsense. If only Mom and Dad had watched *War of the Graveyard Ghouls*, they'd understand this and move her somewhere else. . . .

Some of the residents in wheelchairs were already lined up in the hall, waiting for an aide to take them to the dining room. Jody's heart beat fast as he hurried past, not answering out loud the questions in their eyes. No, you don't know me. I'm not your grandson, not your nephew. No, no, *no* I'm not lying.

He knew he'd probably find a free wheelchair outside the TV lounge. But as he drew closer, the idea of watching even a few minutes of television seized him. Surely something good was on now—a new episode of *Space Base* or even the *Star Power* semifinals. Maybe he'd be in time to see who won junior male vocalist—that little skinny kid from Texas or this week's challenger. Meanwhile, Mom and Dad would check with the nurses about how Grandma's week had gone, then get fussing with her hair and talking about stuff she wouldn't remember. They'd never even miss him. . . .

It was 4:21 (plus an hour) when his parents came looking for him in the lounge. Dad said nothing, just sighed and shook his head.

Jody braced himself for the Lecture. That would

come from Mom, he knew, because for some reason, it was always Dad's job to play good cop, like on TV. Jody had realized that a long time ago.

"You know, Jody, we're very disappointed in you," Mom said at last. He didn't have to be Spodie Masters, Private Eye, to have figured that out. "You said you were going to get a wheelchair. And didn't we ask you to cut back on television?"

"I didn't promise, did I? I said I'd try." His parents exchanged a withering glance and Jody rushed on. "It's just scary here, you know? All those people looking at me, trying to remember if I belong to them. And then there's Grandma—" He broke off with a shrug. "If Uncle Billy ever comes, who will she think *he* is?"

"I know, I know." Dad sounded weary of the conversation and it had barely begun. "It's hard for us, too, seeing her like this. But we just have to believe she's in there somewhere, that these visits make a difference."

"But how can *I* make a difference when she doesn't even know who I am?" Jody blinked away the sudden itching in his eyes. "Anyway, I don't see what's so wrong with sitting here, taking a break."

"You're not just sitting, Joseph Douglas, and you know it." Dad gaped at him as if he'd just told the biggest lie in the world. "You're glued to that stupid screen, watching junk. Whatever's on. We practically had to turn it *off* to get your attention."

"So? I have an inquiring mind. I wanna know stuff." Jody forced a grin.

"Oh, good grief!" Mom rolled her eyes. "Tom, what are we going to do with this boy?"

Dad tugged at his beard. "Well," he said, "I suppose we *could* go back to the point system."

No way, Jody thought. There was nothing more embarrassing than having a chart posted on the refrigerator, telling the whole world how many minutes of TV he'd earned the right to watch. "That's for babies," he blurted. "I promise, I'll be better." His parents looked unconvinced. "Really. I will." Jody checked his watch. "Hey, look, it's almost dinner time. Don't you think we should get Grandma?"

"You should have thought of *that* twenty minutes ago," Dad said, but stepped aside to let Jody pass. Jody wished he could hear what Dad was whispering to Mom. Something about brains and mush and consequences, and it sounded like this time he meant business.

Chapter 4

◎ On the way home from Grandma's, Jody braked and swerved, only narrowly missing the squirrel that shot across his path. With a *click* and a *clack* and a sickening clunk, his bicycle chain slipped from its cogwheel, forcing him to stop short right in front of the cemetery. Why couldn't Dad have just listened to him, understood like Mom had, and agreed to ride home past the park? So what if Dad and his dumb friends had *played* in the cemetery when they were kids? That only showed how weird they were.

Snorting in frustration, Jody dismounted and called to his parents, who were getting farther and farther ahead of him. "Hey, you guys! Stop! Help!"

As his cry echoed off the granite monuments, startled birds seemed to explode from a massive oak, black fireworks against the melting sky. Jody's pulse quickened, but he was sure it was the wind that made tears gather at the corners of his eyes. Were Mom and Dad still so mad about his TV watching that they were simply ignoring him?

With a sigh of resignation, Jody grabbed the rusty handlebars and started walking. His high-top shoes slapped the damp pavement, making soft sucking sounds. Every few feet he stole another sideways peek at the cemetery to reassure himself that nothing was actually lying in wait.

When his parents reached the crosswalk, they finally looked around for him and turned back. Let them be angry. Let them ground him for a month, just as long as they didn't make him pass the rest of the cemetery alone. "Jody, quit it!" he said aloud. "Don't be such a baby!" Then he bent his head low, his safety helmet into the wind.

At last, his parents' bicycles skidded to a stop in front of him. That look of utter frustration flashed again in Dad's eyes, though he said nothing.

"Oh, Tom. You see there?" Mom pointed at the drooping chain. "He was afraid this might happen."

"No problem. I'll have her fixed in a sec."

Jody wished his heartbeat would return to normal, wished his cheeks would decide whether to be hot or cold. He steadied his father's bicycle as well as his own. Mom straddled hers, leaving Dad to fumble with the oily chain. But she was frowning strangely at Jody, cocking her head like a little bird. "What's the matter?" she asked. "You look like you've seen a ghost. That, or you're going to be sick."

"Who, me?" Jody played the innocent. After that scene back at Sunnyview, there was no way he was going to confess what he'd watched last night. No way he'd admit that his imagination was still working overtime. "I-I'm fine. It's just this chain. . . ."

"Watch now, Joe," Dad said, "so *you* can do it next time."

Jody chewed the inside of his cheek, worrying where he'd be the next time. Worrying, too, whether Mom had bought his explanation.

"There. Almost got her." Dad's forehead and cheeks flushed above his beard from the effort of bending over his paunchy belly. When he stood up, the color clashed with the stop-sign red of his helmet.

Jody's pulse eased back toward normal.

"See? Good as new." Dad slapped the two-tone seat as if to prove his point. Jody imagined it sliding down its shaft, the handlebars drooping, and the old balloon tires deflating in the same instant. It could happen, he thought. The way this day was going, *anything* could happen.

"Yeah. Good as new. Thanks." Jody tried to sound like he meant it. But four months was a long time to wait till he got a better one for his birthday. He tried to gauge Mom's reaction; she had such a thing about people being grateful. Had his tone given her another reason to be disappointed in him?

"I don't know *what's* going on with you," she said, and shook her head. "I just get this feeling there's something you're not telling us."

"I-It's nothing. I'm fine, now. Really."

Dad gave an exaggerated shiver. "Brrr. Cold front's coming through. Let's finish this at home, okay, Ellen?"

Flanked by his parents now, Jody noticed that the dreaded graveyard demons seemed to skulk off into the shadows. At last the cemetery gave way to city golf course. What was left of the flutter in Jody's stomach died at once. He scolded himself for having spun fear from thin air.

As they neared home, Jody shivered inside his nylon jacket and glanced over at Dad. His father's jaw was set in a firm, tight line. His eyes seemed to focus somewhere beyond the road.

So what's my consequence? Jody wanted to shout. He wished Dad, Mom—one of them—would just tell him already. Probably what *he* imagined was worse than anything they'd ever come up with. Still, he couldn't stand not knowing.

In the gathering darkness, the houses on Jody's street traced identical silhouettes against the sky. If it weren't for the brass numbers over each front door, it would be easy to mistake one house for another. Mom, however, had already raised the garage door, and the light over his parents' cars cast a welcoming halo.

As Dad stowed their bicycles in the far corner of the cluttered garage, Jody checked his watch. The eerie indigo numbers glowed 6:26. Really 7:26. Ducking past his father without speaking, he made a beeline for the house.

"And where are *you* going in such a hurry?" Dad asked, right behind him.

"Uh, upstairs."

"Uh-huh." Dad winked knowingly. "I bet you couldn't make it through even one day without TV."

"Yes I could. Easy. I could make it through *more* than that—if I wanted to."

Dad raised one eyebrow. "Really? What would you do instead?"

"Play video games."

"Don't you need a TV for that?"

Jody hung his jacket in the mudroom, eyeing his father suspiciously. Surely he wasn't planning to take away TV *and* video games. That was unreasonable, and if Jody could count on Dad for anything, it was for usually being reasonable.

"So?" Dad persisted. "What would you do?"

Jody squirmed. He hated the way his father was looking at him—smug and patient, like he already knew the answer but would wait for it anyway. Jody wished he could recall the list of things Mom always suggested he do whenever he complained about being bored. Instead, he just shrugged.

"I don't understand *why* you hardly ever invite kids over to play."

"Play?" Jody blinked up at his father. "That's for babies."

"Hang out, then. When *I* was your age . . ."

Yeah, yeah, I know. But that was practically fifty years ago! Jody couldn't help tuning him out. He'd heard all about the peculiar things his father used to do, making his bike into a car and using smashed bottle caps as fake money. It sounded pretty dumb. But then, those were the fifties. These were the nineties. Dad should hardly expect kids today to have fun the same way he had. Other fathers—*younger* fathers—wouldn't, Jody thought. They'd do stuff with their kids. Fun stuff. Spend time with them. And bike riding to see Grandma didn't count.

His father nudged his arm. "You're not even listening, are you? Tell me, what would it take to get you off TV?"

"Totally?"

"For two weeks, say. Cold turkey."

Spending time with you. Jody wished he could say the words aloud. But why set himself up for disappointment? If it hadn't happened in eleven-and-a-half years, there was no way it could happen now. And so he blurted the next thing that popped into his mind. "A new bike."

"Hmm. An interesting proposition. Let me check with the boss." Dad's eyes held a hint of amusement as he eased an arm around Jody's shoulder and walked him down the hall to the kitchen.

Mom was unloading the dishwasher. The pots and pans made a terrible racket as she stacked them in the cabinet. She'd asked Jody to do it after lunch but he'd forgotten. Now he flinched at the sound, accepting a twinge of guilt.

"Dad? So . . . ?" Six-twenty-eight, his watch said. Any minute *The Father Muldowney Murders* would be on. He and Dad didn't actually have a deal yet, did they?

"Ellen, I've got an idea I want to bounce off you." Dad turned to Jody. "Why don't you go upstairs for a bit and let us talk?"

"Sure. No problem." Jody waited until he hit the landing before breaking into a run. Closing the door to his parents' bedroom, he grabbed the remote control, flopped on their bed, and cycled through the channels just to make sure he wasn't missing something more exciting. At last he selected his first choice. The familiar theme music, a mixture of clomping footsteps and screeching cats, made him grin. Good. He wasn't too late.

They had to know he'd been watching their television again, though Mom skipped the Lecture and Dad got right to the point. "Here's the deal, Joe. No TV and no video games for the next two weeks, and we get you that new bike."

"An early birthday present," Mom added. "Piece of cake, right?"

"But it's spring break." Jody panicked at the thought.

"Take it or leave it," Dad said.

Jody sighed, wishing he'd had the courage to tell his father what he really wanted—and that it wouldn't cost him a thing. "Okay, I'll take it."

"Good." Dad palmed the remote control. "Guess you won't be needing *this*." Jody couldn't help watching where his father put it—in his underwear drawer. "So," Dad continued, "what are you going to do until bedtime?"

Jody glanced at his watch: 6:52. Which really meant almost 8:00. He had two hours to kill. "It's too late to call anyone," he said, "and besides, it's Easter. Who'd be home? They're probably all off at their relatives'." Jody sighed. "I guess I could read."

"Don't sound so enthusiastic," Dad said.

"Well, what would *you* do?" Jody regretted the question the instant he asked it.

"Me? Oh, that's easy. I'd build forts in the basement, or make up skits. Play cards. And of course there was always Spymaster. That old house on Oneida was full of great hiding places, but I could always find everyone. Not like Billy." Dad smiled at the memories. "Sally and I used to drive him crazy. You know, the poor kid never once made Spymaster. And would you believe *I'm* the only one who never got demoted?" Dad's enthusiasm made Jody squirm. "I never told you about Spymaster? You sure, Joe? It's kind of like hide-and-seek, only—"

"What can I say?" Jody cut in, before Dad really got rolling about the stupid game. "I've had a deprived childhood. No Billys or Sallys to play with, remember?"

Dad shot Mom a warning look, and the veins in his forehead formed a strange, crude V that Jody had never noticed before. Was Dad signaling her not to stir up that old debate about whether to adopt or take in foster kids?

Jody figured if he could get their attention back on him, maybe they wouldn't argue. "Sounds like a baby game, if you ask me," he said. "No way *I'd* ever play it."

"How do you know if you haven't tried it?" Dad

asked. "Too bad I've got to go finish my column. I'd challenge you to a game myself."

Even as Jody rolled his eyes, he realized how easily he might set a trap for his father. "Yeah," he said casually, "it's too bad. Because I bet you anything I could hide someplace where even *you'd* never find me."

"Oh, you do, do you?"

Jody nodded, his face a mask.

"Not on your life, buddy. You're on!" Dad swallowed the bait whole and Jody reeled him in. As the two shook hands, sealing the deal, Jody caught Mom's knowing wink and couldn't help but smile.

". . . four . . . five . . . six . . ."

As Dad's count continued, Jody hit the main floor, his sneakers squealing round the bend, and took the basement stairs two at a time. Surely among all that junk from Grandma's there would be a perfect hiding place.

He opened the door to the storage area. A musty cobwebs-and-damp-boxes smell hit him squarely in the face. He ventured in anyway. A wedge of light from the hallway cut across the concrete floor, guiding his way. He would hide himself so well that the Great Spymaster could look all night and never find him. Jody grinned, imagining his father's frustration at finally being demoted—and in Uncle Billy's shoes for a change. Meantime, Jody intended to enjoy getting more attention than Dad's newspaper column for once.

Surely the count must have been nearing twenty, but

Jody could no longer hear the numbers. He bumped into something hard and low—a trunk, he thought—and fumbled to open the lid. His hands grazed a metal lock. Turning, he groped his way along the wall, dank and cold as a headstone.

Jody shivered. This was the basement; he was just playing a game, and a dumb one at that. Still, he had the strangest feeling that he was not alone, that, somehow, he was being watched. When he finally plucked up his courage and whirled about, two circles glowed like huge bug eyes from the far corner of the room. Jody squinted, and in a blink, they seemed to disappear into the cabinet of Grandma's old-fashioned hulk of a television. Standing as tall as his shoulder and on little carved feet, it looked nothing like the modern compact sets atop his parents' castered VCR stands. Funny—just today at dinner Grandma had asked Dad whether he still had her old TV. "I might be needing it soon," she'd said. Dad, of course, had played along.

Jody drew closer. The guts of the set were gone, and all that remained was the sturdy wooden shell. There was no way anyone would ever be needing *this* thing, he thought. It'd be a miracle if they even made replacement parts anymore. Below where the screen would have been, two fat dials stared back at him. A control panel sporting a wide, black V seemed to grin as if it were alive. As if it were greeting him. Hairs on the back of his neck prickled as the TV face held him, transfixed.

Footsteps thudded overhead. With the hall light on

and the door to the basement stairs ajar, Dad would surely find him now. Desperate for a hiding place, Jody lunged for the set. His blood beat in his ears, burned in his cheeks. Feeling his way, he squeezed through the opening where the screen should have been. Then, huddling in the corner of the cabinet on the chilly concrete floor, he made himself small. Sheltered now and cloaked in shadow, he closed his eyes, willing himself to somehow disappear among the other castaways of Grandma's life.

In a heartbeat, a strange low roaring began in his head. Soon, the static white noise of a cable outage filled his ears. Fighting to overcome a wave of dizziness that made his stomach climb and his thoughts spin, Jody opened his eyes. A dense fog swirled about him. He could barely read the numbers on his glowing watch face. It seemed to lose focus, to fade altogether from view. Blurring, dimming. Then everything went black.

Chapter 5

◎ Maybe Dad had turned the lights off. Jody peered into the darkness. His panic mounted even as he pressed his back against the solid, wooden cabinet. He tried to reassure himself that he was, indeed, where he thought he was. And yet, and yet . . .

The strange static noise persisted, filled his ears. His stomach lurched as if something were pulling him down, down, and away, as if he were being sucked into an invisible drainpipe. If the TV cabinet still surrounded him, he could neither see nor feel it. He opened his mouth to scream, but his voice died deep in his throat.

It made no sense that he could be free-falling. Yet thick fog kept swirling around and past him. With a shiver, he hugged himself to ward off the dampness. From a great distance came searing bits of light mixed with a tinkling of shattering glass. The sparks and noise grew brighter and louder, louder and brighter, with each passing moment, and he realized that, somehow, he was zooming toward both.

All at once, a bright ray pierced the fog. It opened a

hole through which Jody could unmistakably see a hand reach in and begin groping about. Instinctively, he drew his legs up tight against his chest. Even so, whoever it was—because the hand was definitely too small to be Dad's or Mom's—was about to touch Jody's shoe! Scooting backward, he again felt the wooden cabinet and suppressed a gasp.

What was the person looking for? Jody patted the floor and pulled his hand back with a start—and a prick. Instead of damp concrete, he felt short, nubby carpet littered with shards of metal and glass. Taking care not to cut himself, he tried again and discovered a baseball. He nudged it forward and shrank into the farthest corner of the TV set.

"I got it!" a boy said, snatching the ball. "Come on, you guys. Let's get the heck out of here before my mom finds out!"

Jody trembled as a herd of kids thundered past him. A door slammed. From farther away came the sound of some man singing opera over the whir of a kitchen machine.

"T.J.? Is that you?" a woman's voice called.

Jody wondered whether he might have gone mute in the last few minutes. His tongue felt strangely thick and useless. He couldn't have answered even if he'd wanted to. Wherever he was, he knew that he had to get away. Fast.

Climbing out of the wooden cabinet, he found himself in a living room he'd never seen before. A boxy, pea-green sofa and side chair glistened with plastic coverings. Lamps with hanging crystal prisms adorned each end of a painted fireplace mantel.

Jody glanced back nervously at the broken television set. It looked like Grandma's—only without the scratches and dents—and somehow right at home amid the rest of the old-fashioned furniture. What if that woman came in? She'd think *Jody* had smashed it, not those other kids. No way *he* was going to take the blame.

Hurrying off in the direction they'd gone, he found himself in a front entry hall.

"T.J.? I'm talking to you!" This time footsteps followed the woman's voice.

Jody dove for the open door ahead of him. A closet, he thought. But all at once the floor disappeared beneath his feet and he was falling. Grabbing wildly, he connected with a handrail in the near darkness. Surely the woman had heard the clatter! Damp basement smells drifted up the stairs as he, finding his feet again, hurried down them.

Something winked eerily. His watch, he realized, and squinted at the glowing numbers: 88:88. That was weird. It had never done *that* before. But there was no time now to wonder, nor to try resetting it. Besides, it was too dark.

He could do nothing more than blink, letting his eyes adjust, as muted street light sifted in through several high windows. Unlike his own basement, this one had a black-and-white tiled floor. A huge fireplace divided the space into a play area strewn with blocks and trucks and rattletrap furniture, and another area where piles of laundry waited for a turn in the machine. Around the corner, he discovered three small steps leading up to a door.

He imagined what was on the other side—a space, then more steps, leading up to double doors. Maybe a cellar of some kind, like Dorothy was supposed to have gone to in *The Wizard of Oz*. If he was right, then he was out of here, no sweat. After a quick look over his shoulder, he threw back the latch and slipped out of the house. Just as he'd suspected, other doors made a roof overhead. He pushed one open. It squealed for an agonizing moment, then, in merciful silence, let him scramble up into a backyard.

His heart beat in his throat as he paused to get his bearings. He wasn't surprised that it was nighttime, only that it was so much chillier than before. Jody supposed it was that cold front Dad said was coming through. Rubbing at the rising goose bumps on his bare arms, he stole toward the sidewalk.

This wasn't *his* street. Of that, he was sure. Unlike the lookalike box houses and scrawny new trees Jody was used to, this neighborhood boasted elms that must have been there forever and mountain-range houses, all peaks and sloping roofs against a charcoal sky.

And whose house had he just come out of, anyway? Big and brick and sturdy, it looked vaguely familiar, like one of those happy-family houses on TV reruns.

His watch was still blinking 88:88, demanding his attention in a most annoying way. He pressed the reset button, thinking he would guess at the time. But instead of letting him adjust the numbers, the watch simply stopped flashing.

He couldn't worry about that, though. Not now. He had finally spotted several boys, cowering in the long night-shadows in front of the house. His cheeks and ears burned as he drew nearer. Again, he shivered. If only he were wearing a sweatshirt! The others were, along with rolled-up blue jeans, black canvas tennis shoes, and super-short buzzed haircuts. No one *he* knew would be caught dead looking like that.

The dark-haired kid was the first to notice Jody. He stared in a way that made Jody feel as if Jody himself were the strange one. "Where'd *you* come from?"

Jody tried his voice and found it as rusty as the Tin Man's. "O-Over there," he said vaguely, pointing toward the backyard.

"And where in Sam Hill did you get those shoes?" The other kids gathered around to gawk as well. "And that thing on your wrist. What *is* that?"

Hadn't they ever seen leather high-tops and a digital watch before? What was wrong with these kids, anyway? Jody clapped his hand defensively over the watch face and looked down at his shoes. "I-I can't remember where I got them." His voice came out small despite a spark of indignation. Why did it matter what store they'd come from?

The dark-haired kid indicated Jody's wrist. "Looks like something out of the funnies. A Dick Tracy watch, huh? Neat-o."

The others nodded and murmured appreciatively.

Dick Tracy watch? What were they talking about? Jody could feel his own voice slipping away again as he shivered and looked about. "W-Where am I, anyway?" He tried to run the last few scenes of his life backward, like a movie in his mind. Maybe they would all make sense when he replayed them. But he doubted it. "What just happened here?"

"Don't know what happened to *you*," the dark-haired boy said, "but me, I just broke our TV. Smashed it all to smithereens. *Ka-pow!*" He made a cycling motion with his arms. "You should have seen it."

If Jody hadn't heard before how scared the kid sounded, he would have assumed him a braggart. Now he could only stare, trying to figure the boy out. Was he sure Jody *hadn't* seen the TV break? Maybe he'd noticed him inside when he'd reached for the ball.

"See you, T.J.," said one of the other boys, edging away. "I don't want to be around when your mom finds out."

"Me neither. You're in deep Dutch this time. Come on, Jack. Let's get out of here."

Jody supposed those two were brothers because they both hurried off down the sidewalk toward the same house. Maybe *they* didn't believe that lame explanation about where Jody had come from any more than this T.J. kid did.

Watching them go, T.J. folded his arms across his chest as if daring the rest of the group to desert him as well. One boy tossed him something furry, and T.J. put it on his head. Jody gaped in disbelief.

"What *are* you looking at?" T.J. said.

Jody pointed at the striped animal tail hanging down beside T.J.'s ear. He'd seen coonskin caps before in old westerns, of course, but he'd never actually stumbled across one in real life.

"If you want to wear it, all you got to do is ask."

"But I—"

T.J. ignored Jody's protest and plopped the cap on his head. "Got it at Disneyland. You ever been there?"

"Oh, sure. Lots of times. Back when we lived in California."

If T.J. was impressed, he didn't show it. "Bet you weren't there for the grand opening," he said, exhaling on his fingernails, then rubbing them back and forth on what Jody supposed was an imaginary sheriff's badge.

The grand opening? What a liar. That was eons ago. Jody opened his mouth to say so, but the protest wouldn't come.

"Jack's right. We'd better get out of here," the red-haired kid said.

T.J. turned to Jody. "Well? You coming?"

Stunned that he was being invited, Jody swallowed the rising lump in his throat and nodded. But his feet refused to move as the other boys grabbed their bikes off the lawn and pedaled down the well-lit street, calling for T.J. to hurry up.

"*Now* what's the matter?" T.J. said. His hands were on his hips and he looked plainly disgusted.

"D-Do you know me?" Jody asked, touching the cap self-consciously.

T.J. shrugged. "I thought you knew those other guys."

"Well, I don't. I never saw them before in my life. As a matter of fact—"

"Hey, it's okay. Really. As long as you don't rat on me to my mom. Come on."

T.J. tugged at Jody's arm, then dashed off down the sidewalk. Jody, afraid to be left alone, fled after him. Better to be *with* the strange kid, he thought. At least until I figure out where I am.

"No bike, huh?" T.J. asked.

"Not here, anyway."

"Don't you even have a sweater or something?"

Jody shook his head.

"I know! The tree house!" Without so much as checking for traffic, T.J. raced across the street toward an empty wooded lot. Jody followed, hunching his shoulders against the night's chill. The other boys were out of sight now, but T.J. seemed not to notice. Or to care.

Must be late, Jody thought. For sure, almost bedtime. Out of habit, he checked his watch. 88:58. Now the crazy thing appeared to be going *backward*!

"Should have brought my flashlight," T.J. muttered. He held several branches aside, allowing Jody to pass.

Ahead in the gloom, Jody made out the shape of a ramshackle fort in the crotch of a low tree. He doubted that he would have seen it from the street. "Did you build this?" he asked, letting T.J. lead the way up the makeshift ladder. "All by yourself?"

"Me and a couple other kids from around here. We all kind of pal around."

"Pal around?"

"You know. *Do* stuff." T.J. poked his head through a hole in the floor and pulled himself up.

Jody scrambled after him, his teeth chattering like runaway skeletons. The cozy space held a sharp, plywood smell from boards that creaked under their weight. T.J. draped a woolen blanket about Jody's shoulders. It stank and prickled his bare arms, but at least it was warm.

"You're not from around here, are you." It wasn't a question.

"I-I don't think so. But I guess that all depends on where here is."

"What kind of a question is that?" T.J. scoffed. "Here is here. Where else would it be?"

Jody sighed. How could he explain what he himself did not understand?

"What's your name, anyway?" T.J. asked, ignoring Jody's silence.

"Jody."

T.J. snorted. "That's a girl's name."

"Actually, it's Joseph, after my dad's middle name."

"Ha! That's *my* middle name, too. Thomas is my real name, but it's so uppity, don't you think?"

Uppity. That's just what Dad always said about the name Joseph. A tickle began in the pit of Jody's stomach. He wished he could see T.J.'s face better. All that stuck in his mind were dimples and a pointed chin.

"I said it's uppity, don't you think?" T.J. repeated.

"How do you mean?"

"Take your real name, for instance. Joseph what?"

"Douglas."

"See? An old man's name. Jody's a lot better. Hey. You warmer now?"

"Yeah. Thanks." He wondered when T.J. planned to finally face his mother. Did he intend to stay out here all night? "What time do you think it is?" Jody asked.

"Thought you had a watch."

"It's broken, looks like."

"Too bad. When are you supposed to be home?"

"Now, I guess." Jody blinked quickly, glad that T.J. couldn't see his eyes. "I-I'm just not sure where home *is*. How to get there, I mean."

"So, you're lost? That's easy. Just tell me your address."

Jody did, and T.J. shrugged. "Never heard of it. But we could ask my dad. His store delivers all over the city."

"Yeah, but . . ." Jody nodded toward the house. "You sure you want to go back there right now?"

"Uh, maybe not. I see your point."

They sat for several minutes without speaking. Jody

stroked the raccoon tail, trying to clear his mind, to calm his thoughts. "Don't laugh," he said at last, "but I feel like I just dropped in from outer space or something."

"Outer space? You slay me." T.J. shifted around in the fort until Jody could feel the boy's breath on his face.

"I'm not kidding."

"Don't say it. You swear to God and hope to die, and stick a needle in your eye, right? You're what? A Martian? Right here on Oneida Place? Ha! Don't make me laugh."

Something whirred at the back of Jody's brain. He wished he could bring it forward where it might make sense. What was wrong with this kid? Of course Jody wasn't an alien! He supposed he may as well tell T.J. the whole incredible story, because so far, he was getting nowhere, keeping it to himself. What did he have to lose?

"Look," Jody said, "all I know is one minute I was playing this stupid game with my dad. I hid in this old-fashioned TV set. And the next thing I knew, everything got weird and I ended up in your living room inside *your* old-fashioned TV."

"You're crazy. And ours is *not* old-fashioned. It's the latest thing. The wave of the future, Dad says. We've got the biggest antenna on the block, too." T.J. sounded truly indignant.

"Antenna? Nobody has antennas. Satellite dishes, yeah, maybe. But not antennas. How many channels do you get with it, anyway?"

"We're up to four now. Isn't that great?"

"Four?" Jody scoffed. "We've got sixty! Don't you guys get cable or HBO?"

"What's that?"

"Everybody knows what cable is, even if they don't have it. No offense, but are you living in the Dark Ages or what?"

"Define Dark Ages," T.J. said.

"The olden days. You know. Like the sixties."

"The sixties? You mean the *eighteen* sixties?"

"The *nineteen* sixties, dummy," Jody said. *"Everyone* knows that."

T.J.'s hand closed suddenly around Jody's wrist. "That's the olden days to you? God's honest truth?"

Jody nodded.

"But it's nineteen fifty-eitht."

"Nineteen fifty-eight?" A nervous chuckle forced itself from deep in Jody's throat. "No it isn't. It *couldn't* be."

"What do you think I am? Stupid? Think I don't know what year it is?"

"I-I didn't say that, but . . ." Jody struggled for words, drowning in the silence. "Okay, who's president? Who's vice president?"

"Eisenhower and Nixon," T.J. said. "Who did you think?"

"Nixon's *vice* president?" T.J. nodded, but Jody was sure he'd seen reruns of the news clips, showing the guy resigning, something about a cover-up. He even remembered the day all his TV shows were interrupted to air Nixon's *funeral.*

T.J. felt Jody's forehead with the back of his hand. Something about the touch of those fat little fingers sent a sudden chill along Jody's spine.

"Are you sick or something?" T.J. asked. "What did you *think* Nixon was?"

Jody sucked a steadying breath. "Where I come from, he's an ex-*president* . . . a dead one."

"Sure he is."

"He is. Really," Jody insisted, hunkering under the scratchy blanket. His thoughts raced in the darkness, leading to only one conclusion. He allowed it to surface, to form itself into words. It couldn't be, but it *had* to be. Nothing else made any sense. "Don't you see, T.J.? I must have time traveled!"

"Time traveled? Like in that H.G. Wells book?"

"Never heard of it. Or him. But—"

"Then how could you possibly know anything about . . ." T.J.'s voice trailed off, but his disbelief was clear.

Jody paid no attention. What street did T.J. say they were on? Oneida Place, wasn't it? His spine turned to gelatin; he slumped against the wall. "Jeez," he said at last, and heard the awe in his voice, "just like in *Back to the Future*."

"Back to the—what?"

"Never mind. Never mind." If it *was* 1958, the film title would mean nothing to T.J. Jody's heart pounded in his ears as he did some mental math. He tried to imagine what T.J. would look like in almost forty years—with a beard and glasses. "Your last name's Anderson, isn't it?"

"How'd you know? And don't tell me you're psychic."

It was all Jody could do not to blurt out everything else he had suddenly realized—that T.J. was probably around eleven, that he had a big sister named Sally and a little brother named Billy, and a father—yes! Grandpa Anderson, whom Jody had never met—and a mother, whom Jody *had* met and *still* didn't know.

He longed to tell T.J. all this and more: that *his* last name was Anderson, too. But he bit back the words. No matter what his parents thought, Jody had learned *something* from TV—that it could be dangerous for Thomas Joseph Anderson to know the whole truth. To know that Jody was his son.

Chapter 6

If this had been happening on television, Jody would have expected some change in the music—an eerie crescendo perhaps or a chilling echo effect. But now, even as his discovery rushed like white noise through his brain, the world fell silent and it was hard to breathe. He realized, as if through a trance, that T.J. was shaking him by the shoulders. With a heavy tongue, Jody mumbled something he himself could not understand.

"I said 'Hey'! You all right?"

"Sure," Jody managed at last. "Why wouldn't I be?"

"You went white as a sheet, for a minute there. I darn near thought you were gonna pass out on me." The relief in T.J.'s voice was unmistakable. "So, what's the trick? How'd you know my last name, anyway?"

"It's . . . isn't it on the mailbox?"

"Yes, but . . ." T.J. did not finish his thought. They hadn't even gone past the mailbox. Was that what he was thinking? Jody wished he could see his face. Would it be as hard to read as Dad's often was? "Look, no offense," T.J. said at last, "but nobody's going to believe you really time traveled. Maybe Billy will. He'd believe anything but—"

"Do *you* believe me?"

"Oh, sure. Why wouldn't I?" From his tone of voice, though, T.J. may as well have added, "Right, and I still believe in Santa Claus and the tooth fairy, too."

Jody sighed. "Truth is, I can hardly believe it myself."

"Then let's be smart. Don't tell 'em. We could make up a story, like you're an orphan or something. Mom's always taking in foster kids. She's a real softie that way."

Jody realized with a start that T.J. was talking about Grandma—crazy Grandma Anderson. He made her sound like a regular person, nice even. That, he thought, was almost as incredible as his being here in the past to meet her himself.

T.J. rushed on. "We could say your parents died in Chicago and you were taking the bus up here, to live with your grandma—only she died, too. We could look in the paper and pick out the name of some old lady from the death notices, okay?"

"Works for me." Jody couldn't believe how excited T.J. was getting, just thinking up the cover story. He bit back a grin, remembering how Dad got like that, too, whenever he was working on a *real* cover story for the newspaper's Sunday magazine. "So, when should we do it? You planning to stay out here all night or what?"

Before T.J. could reply, Jody's stomach growled embarrassingly. No wonder, he realized with a start. He had hardly eaten a thing at the nursing home and not so much as a bite thereafter. How many hours ago was that? He wished his watch were working properly. But even if it were, what would it prove? He had no idea whether time in the future was standing still or moving on without him—and, if so, at what speed. Again came the insistent grumble. "Did you hear that? I'm *starving*."

"You and me both. Well," T.J. said glumly, "I guess I've got to go back *some*time. But, boy, am I going to be in for it."

"And you still think she'd let me stay?" Jody knew that *his* mother wouldn't if *he* had just broken a TV set.

"Sure. Like I told you, she's a sucker for strays. And she'll probably go easier on me with *you* around."

Jody grunted and tried to reconcile the mother T.J. was describing with the strange and distant grandmother he visited in the nursing home. Reluctantly, he started to shrug the blanket off, but T.J. told him to keep it.

"You're cold," he said, "and you look really pitiful, all wrapped up. Let her see you like that and she'll for *sure* let you stay."

"If you say so." Jody started down after T.J., taking care not to trip or get splinters from the rough cross-pieces nailed into the tree trunk. Beneath the blanket, he glimpsed his watch, which now glowed 88:25. How was he going to explain *that* to T.J.?

A shrill whistle pierced the rustling darkness. T.J. froze near the bushes that fronted the empty lot.

"What's that?" Jody whispered.

"Trouble, probably."

Jody assumed that meant T.J.'s father, scowl in place, standing in the doorway. He tried to conjure up Grandpa's face from old photographs. But all he could imagine was that Thomas Joseph Anderson Senior would probably look too young to be already balding. Jody's stomach churned with wonder and excitement. As if it weren't enough that he'd somehow time traveled through an old television set, now he was about to come face to face for the first time with his very own grandfather!

T.J. bent the branches back as before, then crossed the street. Jody supposed he made a strange sight, scuttling along beside him. "Just let *me* do the talking," T.J. said. "I know how to handle this. Trust me."

As they made their way up the front walk, Jody noticed that ANDERSON was indeed spelled out in silver letters on the mailbox by the door. His pulse raced— *Grand*pa, *Grand*pa, *Grand*pa—as the door loomed. T.J. heaved it open.

Instead of T.J.'s father, a slender woman with wavy blond hair awaited them in the foyer. She wore a flowered apron with sleeves, with a bow tied in front, and brandished a long wooden spoon. Jody braced himself, worried that she might whack T.J. with it. Parents in the olden days sometimes did that, he'd heard. But as he drew closer, he noticed that the bowl end was coated with chocolate.

"Where've you been, Teej? I've been whistling my fool head off for you," she said.

"I was out checking the fort. And look who I found living there. His name's Jody."

Jody swallowed the lump in his throat, trying to work up not only the right words but the breath to get them out. His cheeks went hot with shame at T.J.'s lie, but it couldn't be helped. In the end, he said nothing, just avoided Mrs. Anderson's—Grandma's—eyes.

"P.U.!" Mrs. Anderson plucked at the moldy blanket. Her face wrinkled up with a strange blend of distaste and concern. "You must be mighty cold to welcome a wretched thing like that." She made a soft, clucking sound with her tongue. "Let's get you out of there and into a warm bath." She placed her hand on his forehead as if to detect a fever and looked deep into his eyes. Her directness sent a shiver down his spine. "Do I know you?"

Jody's head shook mechanically, as if by its own will.

"We've never met? Are you sure?"

"Yes. I mean, no, ma'am. Never. You and me, never met." *Now* who was gabbling nonsense?

Mrs. Anderson narrowed her gaze, shook her head. "I don't know. You have a familiar look about you. I just can't put my finger on it."

Jody's jaw went slack and his mouth dry in the same instant. Afraid to look at her, he could only shrug in reply. Dad had always claimed that when he was young, she was practically a mind reader. Did she really have some kind of secret powers?

"You must have him confused with some other kid, Ma," T.J. piped up. "He's new in town."

Mrs. Anderson cocked her head, seemingly still unconvinced. "Never mind. It will come to me. You go hop in that tub, young man. And when you get out, we'd better have us a little talk."

T.J. looked sideways into the living room at the broken TV screen. The guilt on his face was easy reading, but Mrs. Anderson seemed too busy fussing about Jody and his bath to even notice. T.J. fidgeted with his hands for several long moments, then finally blurted, "W-What did you want me for, Ma?"

"To lick the spoon and beaters, if you want. Billy and Sally already got to the bowl." She shrugged apologetically.

Surely she'd heard the sound of shattering glass, Jody thought. Even if she *had* been in the kitchen with the electric mixer and a radio going full blast, there was no way she could have missed it.

T.J. hung his head and nudged his sneaker along the carpet. "I-I've got to tell you something, Ma," he said.

"Yes, dear?" Her clear blue eyes blinked, bright and expectant.

"We . . . somebody . . . I—I'm not sure who, really—broke the TV. Smashed it. Playing ball in the house."

Mrs. Anderson drew in a silent breath. Her eyes widened, and she seemed to grow two inches. Jody cringed in sympathy, as if he himself had been part of the misadventure, which, in a way, he had.

After pausing long enough to count to ten in every

language Jody had ever heard of, Mrs. Anderson at last tipped T.J.'s chin up. "What a lot of courage that took to tell me," she said, picking her way carefully around the words as if they were mine fields. "I'm really proud of you."

"Y-You're not angry?" T.J.'s voice, Jody's thoughts.

Mrs. Anderson laughed. "Angry? I'm *furious!*" Her lips went white around the word. Jody had no doubt that she meant it. "But what can I do when you go and tell the truth?" She pretended to shake his shoulders in exasperation.

"That's it? No punishment?" T.J. asked.

"I didn't say *that*. There will be no TV, of course, until you can pay the repairs. But that goes without saying, doesn't it?"

T.J. nodded dumbly.

Jody realized that his own mouth was hanging open and quickly clapped it shut. What an *incredible* way for a mother to behave—*any* mother, but especially this one, his grandmother. Still, poor T.J. That sounded like no TV for a lot longer than the two weeks he'd bet with Dad in the future. *Which is actually now my past*, Jody thought, suddenly confused, *although I'm not even born yet.*

"No more *Gunsmoke*? No more *Wyatt Earp*?" T.J. wailed, making Jody wonder fleetingly what other shows T.J. would be missing—and whether Jody might have already seen the reruns on cable TV. "How much do you think it will cost, Mother?"

Mrs. Anderson shrugged. "I'd guess ninety to a hundred dollars."

T.J. groaned. "I can never save that much. Never in a million trillion years."

Mrs. Anderson eased her arm around his shoulder. "Slow and steady wins the race," she said. "Upstairs with you now. Go fetch some towels for Jody and run him that bath."

T.J. started for the steps but turned back. "Does Dad know about the TV?"

His mother nodded. "And he's got one of his headaches, so keep the noise down, hear me?'

Jody wasn't sure whether she was talking to him or to T.J. "Yes, ma'am," he said.

He hit the stairs after T.J. and gaped at the massive carved bannister that led up to the second floor. The first door to his right was ajar. Peeking in, he could see a boy about six years old playing with some large wooden building blocks.

"That's Billy," T.J. said. "He won't bother you."

The name *Sally*, fancy stitched in rainbow-colored threads, hung inside a wooden hoop on the closed door across the hall.

"How old's your sister?" Jody asked.

"Thirteen. And she *will* bother you. Take my word for it."

Jody wished suddenly that he'd known Uncle Billy and Aunt Sally in the future. It would have made these first glimpses more interesting, more memorable, somehow.

"Shhh!" T.J. hissed, pointing at another closed door, behind which, Jody assumed, Mr. Anderson was resting. Sneaking past it, he turned left with the hall, grabbed a couple of towels from a linen closet, and ushered Jody into the bathroom. "Take your time. I'll go fix up your bed."

"But she didn't say I could—"

"She will. Don't worry," T.J. said. "She likes you. I can tell."

After T.J. had gone, Jody locked the door and ran the water. Normally he would have taken a shower, but since T.J.'s mother had said *bath*, he figured maybe something was wrong with the showerhead. Dropping his clothes on the chilly tile floor, he climbed into the tub, still wearing his watch. It was waterproof, after all, even if it *was* behaving strangely. Now it said 88:05. He supposed twenty minutes could have passed since he'd last checked. But why did it insist on running backward?

Easing down, he let the hot water inch over his belly. Jody Anderson, a time traveler! And friends with his father to boot. His head was still spinning with the evening's amazing events. Never mind *how* he'd gotten here. Or why. The real question was, how was he going to get home?

T.J. sure made it tempting to want to hang out in the past for a while, though. Even as a kid, Jody thought with grudging admiration, Dad sure had a way with stories. Just a few minutes with T.J. had him almost believing he *was* an orphan from Chicago. And it *would* be kind of cool, getting to know his grandfather and his aunt and uncle. Were they all going to be as understanding about the broken TV as Mrs. Anderson had been? Did they even know yet?

Jody couldn't help but wonder whether T.J.'s mother was really as nice and normal as she seemed. With her apron and lick-the-spoon routine, she could have been one of those black-and-white-TV moms come to life. The punishment she'd decided on didn't seem to Jody nearly as crushing as it did to T.J. A hundred dollars was almost the same as a couple of video games. But by the way T.J. had carried on, it may as well have been a baseball player's multimillion-dollar salary.

Jody slopped the washrag over his face and slipped further into the water. Could this all be some bizarre test to see whether Jody really could keep his bet with Dad? Probably not. Even if T.J. had another TV set in his room, Jody doubted that he'd disobey his mother by turning it on.

Did his own parents know that he was gone yet? Had they called the police? Jody could imagine how frantic Mom would be. Once, he'd wandered off in Penney's and she'd finally found him in the mall by Fanny Farmer's, his nose pressed up against the glass candy case. He'd never seen her eyes so red and puffy. She was probably that way now.

His watch beeped then, startling him from his thoughts. 87:59. For some reason, it seemed to be counting *down*, working just like the timer on his mother's stove. That meant he had eighty-seven hours and fifty-nine minutes. Until what?

He swallowed the rising lump in his throat. And as a sudden draft passed through the room, he shivered. He had to get back. And soon. He was the only kid his parents had—or ever would have, to hear those two talk. No matter how interesting it might be hanging out here with T.J. and his family, this would have to be a quick visit. Nothing more.

Chapter 7

Someone's knock, sharp and insistent, echoed off the bathroom's tiled floor. Jerking upright, Jody reached for the towel on the toilet seat, stood up, and wrapped it about his waist. Whoever was making all that racket was sure to awaken T.J.'s father. That was the last thing Jody needed now—getting off on the wrong foot with the man. *What if he makes me go to some orphanage, like I saw on TV? Then how will I get back home?* Again came the loud knocking.

"Shhh!" he hissed. "I'm coming. I'm coming." Flicking the latch, he opened the door a crack.

Looking down at him with great disdain was a tall, pony-tailed blonde. Her chest, rather lumpy and uneven beneath her sweater, wasn't all that far from Jody's eye level, making it hard not to stare. "Who are *you*?" she demanded.

Jody forced his gaze upward. "Jody An-Andrews." He hoped she didn't notice him stumble over his last name. "T.J.'s friend."

"You're sleeping over?"

"I-I don't—"

"No fair. I never get a sleepover." She pursed her lips and folded her arms across her chest. "Well, don't just stand there. Hurry up. I need to set my hair."

Jody bobbed his head quickly and relocked the door. T.J. was right; she was going to be a bother. Hurriedly, he pulled his Milwaukee Brewers T-shirt on, along with his jeans and shoes. After remembering to hang his towel up—Mom was always nagging him about that—he started off to find T.J.

Sally, still waiting in the hall, pressed herself against the wall and made a face as he passed. She acted as if he had just bathed in sewage. "Wait here a minute," she said, then disappeared into the bathroom. "Eeeeeeuuu-uuw!" Her high-pitched squeal hurt Jody's ears. "Didn't anyone ever teach you to empty the bathtub and scrub away all your scum?"

"Scum?" What was she talking about?

Sally poked her head out, crooked her finger at him, and motioned toward the bathtub. "S-C-U-M, as in pond. What are you, spoiled or something?"

As the water ebbed, gurgling and swirling toward the drain, it left behind a distinctly dingy ring. "I-I'm sorry," he stammered. "I don't ever take baths."

"I can see that," Sally said.

"No, I mean . . ." Jody's cheeks burned. "I *bathe*, but not in tubs."

"Don't tell me. Let me guess. In toilet water?" Sally clicked her tongue, regarding him as if he were some life form lower than an amoeba.

What a way to treat company! Jody tried not to glare back at her. "What I mean is, I take showers. Really. I didn't even know bathtubs *got* like that. But, hey, if you want me to—"

"Never mind," she snapped. "Just get out of here. I'll do it myself." She looked as if she might burst into tears at any moment, though Jody had no idea why.

"It's just a little soap and . . . and . . . well, whatever. You don't have to cry about it."

"What do *you* know?" Sally said. "What do you know about *any*thing?" With that, she shoved him backward, out the door. He could hear the latch slide into place. "Easter vacation with no TV," she muttered to herself. "Great, just great. And *T.J.* gets to have a friend over. Aaaargh! Any other kid would get a spanking, but not her precious little T.J. Oh, no. Not him."

Jody stared at the closed door, stunned at what Sally had just revealed. That it was Easter vacation here, too. That the Andersons apparently had only one television. And that Sally wasn't exactly crazy about having T.J. for a brother. If that was the way *all* sisters felt, maybe Jody wasn't missing anything in not having one, after all. Tiptoeing past Mr. Anderson's room, he headed down the hall.

"Psst, Jody. In here." T.J. waved him into the room next to Sally's and shut the door. He stared at Jody's T-shirt and frowned. "Were you wearing that before? Really? I can't believe I didn't notice. What're the Milwaukee Brewers?"

"A baseball team, dummy." Jody winced at what he'd just called T.J.—his *father*—and realized that he'd called him a dummy earlier, too. Before he'd known who T.J. really was. It was a wonder the kid let him get away with it.

"You're the dummy. It's the Milwaukee *Braves*. Ask anyone."

Jody shook his head. "Atlanta Braves."

T.J. pointed to a pennant on his wall. "Milwaukee. Think I don't know who won the last World Series? Ever heard of Warren Spahn? Ever heard of Hank Aaron?"

"What do *you* think?" Jody didn't have to be a big baseball fan to have heard of Hammerin' Hank. He bet even his *mother* knew who he was—and she *hated* baseball. Still, if T.J. was expecting him to rattle off the top of his head all Hank Aaron's stats, he was talking to the wrong guy. The closest Jody ever came to team sports was wearing their T-shirts or hats.

"So?"

"So, I think the Braves *move*," Jody said, "but don't ask me when. Sometime in the sixties, maybe."

T.J. just shook his head.

"I'm not kidding."

"Okaaaay," T.J. said slowly, drawing the word out, "let's pretend you're not. What else do you know? Do they win the pennant this year, too?"

When Jody shrugged, T.J. grinned smugly as if to say, "See why I don't believe you?"

Suddenly, Jody wished that he'd paid more attention in the future to Scott's constant yammering about baseball every morning at the bus stop. It was amazing how much somebody could learn just from collecting trading cards. Now *there* was a thought. "Hey," Jody said, "you got any good cards?"

T.J. moved aside a section of newspaper, opened the top drawer of his desk, and, with a sweeping gesture, invited Jody to see for himself. Jody's eyes grew wide at the sight of so many famous players' cards tossed carelessly into the drawer. The one time he'd gone to Scott's house, he'd been educated quickly about not bending corners and storing everything in hard plastic sleeves.

"You really ought to take better care of them," Jody said softly. "Someday they're gonna be worth something."

T.J. scowled.

"Who knows?" Jody continued. "You might even want to give them to your kid."

T.J. slammed the drawer. "No way *I'm* having a kid."

"Why not?"

"Because I'm not a girl, silly. Don't you know anything?"

More than you do, I'll bet, Jody thought—not that he wanted to end up teaching nineties health ed stuff to his father in the fifties. "T.J.!" He rolled his eyes in exasperation. "After you're married, I mean. What about then?"

"Me? Get married? You've got to be kidding. Girls have cooties."

T.J. wrinkled his face in disgust, leading Jody to assume that whatever cooties were, he didn't want to have them. But it was all too strange to even consider that as an eleven-year-old, his father hadn't wanted to get married *or* have a kid. Have *him*. And yet he had done it. Could whatever Jody might say or do here somehow change that, somehow threaten his own existence? Maybe getting to know T.J. wasn't such a great idea after all. . . .

"Anyway," T.J. was saying, "you can sleep over there." He indicated an unrolled sleeping bag in front of the closet.

"Boys?" Mrs. Anderson's voice came from the hall. "May I come in?"

T.J. opened the door. His mother left it ajar and regarded Jody kindly. Still, something about her gaze seemed to bore right through him like a laser aimed straight at his brain. How could she possibly know him? Even though Jody scoffed at the thought, his knees went weak and his stomach knotted.

"Now," she said, "how about telling me why you'd be living in a tree house."

"He's an orphan," T.J. blurted.

She quieted him with a snap of her fingers. "I asked Jody."

Jody looked sideways at T.J. and tried to iron the wrinkles out of his story. "I-I didn't know where else to go and . . . and I was just wandering around the neigh-borhood and found it."

Mrs. Anderson frowned, cocking her head in a searching way that reminded him of his own mother.

Jody hurried on. "See, I was coming up here to live with my grandma, but she died and—" he broke off, mustering the most pitiful expression he could imagine. Something like a cross between Charles Dickens's Oliver and that ragamuffin Jimmy in the Walt Disney film *Pollyanna*.

Mrs. Anderson reached out to touch his shoulder. "I think maybe we should call the county welfare office," she said.

"No!" T.J. and Jody spoke as one.

Jody's pulse raced ahead of his thoughts. What were the lines from that old movie he'd seen so many times on cable TV? A sound bite, that's all he really needed. "I mean, please don't, ma'am," he begged. "My daddy grew up in an orphanage and he said it was a terrible place. Just terrible. He wouldn't want me to go there. I know he wouldn't." The kid in the movie had said *turrible*, but Jody didn't think he could pull off the drawl with a straight face.

"Surely there must be other relatives who could take you in," she said. "Didn't anyone come to the funeral?"

Jody looked to T.J., panic rising in his throat. But T.J. was leaning over his desk, reading the comics or something. Of all the times not to be paying attention!

"You *did* go to her funeral, didn't you?"

"Well, I . . ." Jody felt as if he were drowning in lies. "What I meant to say is . . ."

"She was cremated," T.J. cut in, folding the newspaper in half and offering it first to Jody, then to his mother. "See? He was just looking for this."

Jody frantically scanned the tiny print under the name *Aurelia V. Smith*, beside T.J.'s thumb. She had died Friday at the age of seventy-three, leaving no known survivors.

T.J.'s mother raised an eyebrow.

"The newspaper didn't know about me," Jody rushed to explain.

"On account of there being nobody else to tell them," T.J. added.

"I see. Well"— she laid the newspaper on the bed —"I suppose it wouldn't hurt to let you spend the night, it being vacation and all. Just let me check with T.J.'s father. And we can make that call in the morning."

T.J. wriggled at the news, but Jody steeled his own relief. Mr. Anderson might still say no, and what would happen once they called the county welfare office?

T.J. nudged him, and he found his voice. "Thank you, um, ma'am. I'd really appreciate it."

"Is it okay if we fix a snack?" T.J. asked.

Mrs. Anderson nodded. "The beaters are still waiting for you, and there's some leftover ham from supper," she said. "Just see you clean up your mess."

"We will." T. J. grinned at Jody. "Last one to the kitchen is a rotten egg."

Mrs. Anderson stepped aside, touching a finger to her lips. Though the boys stole from the room, they broke into a thundering run near the bottom of the stairs, with

T.J. in the lead. "See?" he said. "I knew she'd let you stay."

"Only if your dad says okay," Jody reminded him. "And only overnight."

T.J. looked momentarily glum. "Well, we'll worry about that tomorrow, huh?"

I'm already worrying, Jody thought, but nodded agreeably. How was he going to get home? If he stayed here long enough to learn more about his father, could he be risking ever going home at all?

T.J. seemed not to sense any concern, however, and brightened when he opened the refrigerator. "So, what's it gonna be? Ham? Baloney? Peanut butter?"

"Peanut butter and brown sugar!" Jody blurted without thinking.

T.J. spun about. "Are you kidding me? This is amazing! We must be the only people in the known world who eat that. What are the odds?"

Any reply died in Jody's throat. He shrugged, trying to appear nonchalant. Meantime, his heart was beating like a whole parade of snare drums. If he didn't watch out, he was going to trip up, say something he shouldn't, make it impossible to go home—at least, home as he knew it. There was no telling how T.J.'s learning the whole truth about Jody might change things—for them both.

"I mean, *really*!" T.J. prodded.

"Where I come from, all the kids eat it," Jody lied.

"Neat-o." T.J. uncapped a jar of peanut butter and

plucked something that looked like a small shower cap off the canister of brown sugar.

All the while, Jody chided himself for being so careless. From now on, he promised, I'm going to think before I talk. Just like Dad always tells me to. He grinned at the irony of using his father's advice to stay one step ahead of T.J.—which was going to be no easy task. Already he could tell that the kid was no dummy.

Chapter 8

Mrs. Anderson tucked the covers so tightly around T.J. that he looked like a mummy. "You're way past your bedtime, Teej," she said, and paused to wind his Woody Woodpecker alarm clock. The cartoon character's gloved hands pointed to the nine and the eleven, almost—making it nine-fifty-five.

"You're sure Mr. Anderson is okay about me staying over?" Jody asked.

"Absolutely, dear. He said to tell you he's looking forward to meeting you tomorrow, when he's feeling better." Her hair cascaded about T.J.'s face as she leaned over and kissed his forehead.

Jody tried to imagine Mrs. Anderson—*Grandma*—tucking him in, too. Did she have a way of warding off bad dreams the way his own mother had? Jody's eyes burned suddenly, and he pressed his cheek further into the folds of his pillow. If only going home from *this* sleepover were as easy as calling Mom in the middle of the night to come get him. From the mounded pillow, he peeked again at T.J.'s mother.

She frowned, and in the same instant, Jody's watch

beeped. She glanced about as if looking for the source. Jody shivered at the realization that she had practically heard the tone before it had even sounded. He checked beneath his covers in time to see the numbers switch from 87:00 to 86:59.

"What was that?" Mrs. Anderson asked.

Jody fumbled to unbuckle the band, then swept the watch toward the bottom of his sleeping bag with his foot. "I didn't hear anything. Did you, T.J.?"

"Nope, not a thing."

Mrs. Anderson continued to stare at Jody in that unnerving way she had. He felt as if an invisible weight were sitting on his chest, crushing the breath right out of him. At last, she shrugged, mumbling something Jody could not understand. "Well, sweet dreams, you two."

As she closed the door, Jody sighed with relief. At least for now, he was safe from any intuition she might have about him. Still, he worried what she would do if she were to realize who he was. All the more reason to make the best of whatever time he might have with T.J. . . . .

Jody tried to concentrate as T.J. babbled on and on about school and the kids in the neighborhood. But he was losing ground fast. All he could think about was the broken TV, how he was going to get home again, and whether Mrs. Anderson might somehow sense who he was before then. Before Jody knew it, T.J. wound down abruptly as if someone had just removed his batteries.

Jody sank into a fitful sleep, awakened by strange creakings and tappings at the window. Once roused, he lay stiff and still, worrying what the new day would bring. Would the Andersons call the welfare worker right away, or would they at least let him stay till afternoon? If so, what would he and T.J. do without television and video games and movie rentals?

His watch, still at the bottom of his sleeping bag, beeped again at 82:00—three-forty-five, by Jody's calculations. He felt as if he would jump out of his skin, wondering what it all meant, how it would end. At last, he crept downstairs, teeth chattering in the darkness, and stood before the TV. His heart slammed against his ribs at the sight of the grinning face of dials below the broken screen. The crazy thing seemed to be taunting him, somehow, as if it knew something that Jody didn't.

Whatever it was, he intended to find out. Dropping to his hands and knees, he gingerly felt inside the cabinet for slivers of glass. There were none. Someone must have vacuumed. Thoughts of what tomorrow might bring pressed hard against his heart. There was no way he could allow himself to end up stuck in the past, living in an orphanage. Not when he had waiting for him in the future two basically fine parents. So what if one of them *did* work too much?

"Try to go home, *now*, this very minute," a small voice whispered.

Without even saying good-bye to T.J.?

Jody hesitated, but the decision came, already made. He knew there were too many ways to muck up the future if he stayed. Steeling his resolve, he climbed inside the TV and made himself small. Then, closing his eyes, he waited expectantly. Nothing happened. Maybe he had to say something, like Dorothy did in *The Wizard of Oz*. Feeling more desperate than foolish, he whispered, "There's no place like home. There's no place like home."

Nothing.

With a sigh, Jody hugged his knees to his chest and fought back tears. Now what was he going to do? After several minutes, a toilet flushed upstairs. No one must find him here, inside the TV. They'd think he was crazy—maybe send him to a mental hospital like in *One Flew Over the Cuckoo's Nest*! At last the noisy pipes calmed. In the eerie silence of the great brick house, he dragged himself out of the TV and back to bed.

But there was no way he could sleep. Soon, he heard the shower running. Did all the Andersons get up this early? If so, he would never last long in this family.

Jody figured he must have finally dozed off, because when T.J.'s door groaned, he bolted upright, blinking and breathless. Sunlight pierced the curtains. When no one came in, Jody whispered, "Who's there?"

"It's me, Billy." The younger boy peered around the door, then inched closer. He was still wearing pajamas, baggy flannels in red plaid. His hair stuck out like porcupine quills. *Like mine*, Jody thought in astonishment. "Who are you?" the boy asked.

"My name's Jody. I'm . . . I'm a friend of T.J.'s."

Billy tilted his head, first one way then the other. "I never seen you before."

"That's because I'm new around here."

"Oh." Billy sat down crosslegged on the sleeping bag, regarding Jody with round-button eyes. "Are you going gofering with me and Teej?"

"I-I guess so." Not that he knew what "go-for-ing" was. Some kind of delivery job, maybe.

"You can be water boy, then," Billy said.

Jody held his face in neutral, playing along, although now the boy really did have him wondering.

Billy started for the door, then turned. "See you at breakfast, okay?"

Jody nodded. Tiptoeing over to T.J.'s bed, he stared hard, as if he could wish T.J. awake. Maybe he *didn't* believe that Jody had time traveled, but at least he would listen and not give him away.

Jody sniffed at his own clothes. His Brewers T-shirt was going to really stink if he didn't change it soon. Sally would be sure to point *that* out.

"T.J., psssst!" Jody touched the boy's shoulder and T.J. sprang awake.

He blinked wide-eyed as if Jody were a ghost, then half-yawned, half-laughed. "Oh yeah. The TV time traveler. I thought I dreamed you up for a minute there."

"What's gofering? When are we going? Is it a job or . . . ? What do I wear? Got something that'll fit me?"

"Whoa. Slow down, will you?" T.J. took his time

getting out of bed, but at last he tugged a storage box out and began rummaging through its contents. "Here. These ought to work." He handed Jody a pair of funny-looking jeans and a hooded sweatshirt, obviously hand-me-downs intended for Billy. "Come on," he said. "Hurry up. We've got to eat and get out of here, before Mom makes that call. I'll tell you everything once we get to the cemetery."

The *cemetery!* At the very word, goose bumps skittered down Jody's arms. What did T.J. intend to do *there*? If only Jody had paid attention to his father's glowing accounts of the good old days. . . .

Turning his face away to hide his alarm, Jody wriggled into the worn clothes. It seemed terribly important, suddenly, not to wimp out. But the cemetery, of all places! His stomach churned at the thought. There had to be someplace better to do this gofering thing.

Maybe at one of those other kids' houses. They could even watch TV there, if T.J. wanted to. Jody wouldn't tell. And he'd settle for any old show, too—whatever they wanted to see—as long as it meant getting out of going to a creepy graveyard.

Downstairs, T.J.'s mother had a full breakfast of scrambled eggs, bacon, cinnamon toast, and orange juice waiting for them. She told them that Mr. Anderson had already gone to work at his grocery store, feeling only slightly better than the night before.

Though Jody mumbled how sorry he was to hear that, inwardly he rejoiced at the news. Mr. Anderson couldn't very well send some poor orphan away until he'd at least met him, could he?

Mrs. Anderson flitted between the stove and the table, waiting on the boys. "What a glorious day this is, isn't it?" she chirped. "Look at that sunshine. I'm so glad it's nice for you boys, it being vacation and all." She smiled warmly at Jody, watching him eat. "Good. You've brought your appetite. I love cooking for healthy eaters. Glad you're here, Jody." She acted as if she had forgotten entirely about making that phone call.

Jody and T.J. exchanged a puzzled glance. Neither spoke. By the time Jody had eaten his fill, he hardly minded the scowl that Sally shot him across the table. He had never received this kind of treatment at his other home, that was for sure. There, breakfast usually consisted of cold cereal or microwaved waffles.

"Well," Mrs. Anderson said, wiping her hands on her apron, "what are you boys going to do this morning?"

T.J. shot Jody a warning look. "Oh, I don't know. Probably go to the park for a while," he said, "and see who's there. Maybe play some ball."

"You're taking Billy, aren't you?"

T.J. nodded and rose to clear his dishes. When Billy did, too, Jody followed their lead.

"Be back by lunchtime and stay out of trouble," Mrs. Anderson called as they headed out the back door and into the cluttered garage.

Her warning eased Jody's mind a bit about the cemetery. Maybe they wouldn't go there after all. But it still seemed strange that she hadn't mentioned calling the county welfare office. Not that Jody was going to remind her. Maybe something was *already* starting to go wrong with her memory, he thought.

"Go get that mayonnaise jar," T.J. told Billy. "And don't break it."

Though Billy stuck his tongue out at his brother, he did as T.J. ordered.

"You take the watering can, Jody. And I'll go whistle for the guys." T.J. poked his head out the service door and, through his fingers, blew two shrill blasts, followed by a pause, then another two.

"Are you sure this is going to be okay?" Jody asked.

"Trust me. I always have the best ideas, don't I, Billy?"

The same words from anyone but T.J. would have sounded like bragging. But from him, Jody thought, they were more a statement of fact. Even so, Billy only shrugged. T.J. whistled again. From somewhere down the street came a similar whistle in reply.

"Sounds like Peaches," T.J. said. He stuffed a pair of work gloves into his back pockets. "Come on. We'll meet him over there."

Over *where*? Jody wondered, finally grabbing the watering can off the workbench. When he glanced about, he was surprised to see a shiny red Schwinn bicycle propped in the corner. It looked strangely familiar, except for a tin can taped to the rear fender. Drawing closer, he inspected the contraption. He wasn't sure why the can had a hole in the bottom or why it was filled with pounded-flat bottle caps. But he *was* sure of two things. That bike would survive for thirty-something years. And it would be the same one that Jody was trying to get rid of before his twelfth birthday!

"Cool bike, isn't it?" T.J. beamed and patted the two-tone seat fondly. "You can ride it later if you want."

"Thanks, but . . . ," Jody said. "That's okay."

"Come on," Billy whispered. "We got to get out of here before a little bird tells her."

T.J. nodded but didn't explain as he shooed Jody and Billy out of the garage. They turned right, away from the house, and wove through the neighborhood of grand old trees and houses until they came at last to a golf course.

"This way," T.J. said, cutting across the fairway.

The grass squooshed underfoot. Jody eyed his sneakers with dismay. If T.J.'s mother was anything like Jody's, she was certain to consider coming home with muddy shoes "trouble"—and he definitely wanted to stay on her good side.

Home. Jody started at the thought. This was not his home. And if he knew what was good for him, he had better guard against getting too comfortable.

"Not much farther now," T.J. said. "The cemetery's right past the sandtrap. Over there."

Somehow that knowledge didn't ease Jody's mind. Stalling for time, he surveyed the gentle grade of the golf course. A row of firs veered off toward the street. Ahead, a great, gnarly oak imprinted the sky with its black lace pattern. A shudder worked its way along Jody's spine, though he could not imagine why. There was something about that tree, something *familiar*, he thought. But what? He started toward it as if entranced.

Chapter 9

◉ The morning air crackled across the golf course as if each leaf, each twig, were electrified. Some unseen force seemed to propel Jody forward.

"Hey," T.J. called, "you're going the wrong way."

Powerless to explain, Jody ignored him. Mud sucked at his sneakers. It seemed that the great tree was pulling him closer until, at last, he was within reach. The other kids' stares could not keep him from touching the rough, gray furrows of bark with a kind of reverence born of distant memory. The gesture reminded him somehow, crazily, of the way T.J. had patted his bicycle seat.

And it came to him then, in a rush of goose flesh and icy prickles at the back of his neck, what this place was—why he knew it—and what it would become. He steadied himself against the sturdy trunk that would be a living marker through eternity. Squinching his eyes, he tried to picture at its foot the smooth granite headstone that he'd visited in the future—the one bearing the inscription *Thomas Joseph Anderson, 1914–1978.*

Spooked by the memory, he turned and bolted. From

the depths of his pocket, where he'd decided to hide it, Jody's watch beeped. He figured it would say 75:00, if last night's calculations were correct; that would translate into about ten forty-five.

"What's the matter with *you*? You look like you seen a ghost." T.J. tugged at Jody's arm. "Come on. It's just a dumb old tree."

That's what *you* think. But Jody said nothing. What good would it do to tell T.J. and Billy what year their father would die? They'd be all grown up by then.

Besides, there was no way either of them could understand any of this. Not when Jody himself barely could. It was just starting to sink in that the graves of T.J.'s father and so many others—that a whole *cemetery*!—would someday eat up this golf course. People would come here not to play a game but to remember and to cry while visiting the dead. Unbelievable. Which only made Jody wonder more what he, T.J., and the others were doing here now.

Biting back his questions, he followed T.J. and Billy away from the tree, across the rest of the fairway, and into the adjacent cemetery. Why weren't either of them scared? True, in the sunlight, with the shadows mere puddles around the headstones, the place didn't seem quite as menacing as it had on the ride from the nursing home. Even so, Jody scurried along, wishing he were safely back in the future, watching this happen on TV.

From behind one of the tombstones came a shrill double whistle. T.J. echoed the signal. The lanky kid with buzzed blond hair sauntered out into the open. His pockets were bulging strangely, and he looked most pleased with himself.

"I found him, T.J.! Already! Can you believe that? I hardly had to search at all," he said. "The main hole's over in Soldier's Lot, behind Addison Gatley. M–23, I think."

T.J. grinned broadly. "That's great, Peaches! Come on!"

Billy raced ahead, clutching the mayonnaise jar to his chest. T.J. and Peaches jogged after him, but Jody hung back. Dread seemed to root him to the spot.

"Whatsa matter with the new kid?" he heard Peaches ask.

"You mean, Jody? He's just shy is all. He's okay."

Jody rolled his eyes. Just because he didn't like playing in cemeteries, it didn't mean that he was shy. Still, he supposed he should be grateful. At least T.J. hadn't guessed that he was afraid—or, if he did, at least he didn't say so aloud.

"Come on, Jody!" Billy waved for him to come, and Jody forced himself forward, fighting the stuffy feeling in his throat.

When he reached the boys at last, Peaches was pulling chunks of rock from his pockets, and T.J. was racing around with them, covering up small holes that dotted a field of identically shaped white granite gravestones. None of the markers had dates—only old-fashioned names and some kind of letter-and-number code.

Overhead a flag licked at the breeze. A robin, fat and muddy-breasted, touched down between the neat rows, cocked its head, and eyed T.J. reproachfully.

Jody set his watering can on a stone bench inscribed with a dedication to the Grand Old Army of the Republic. "Wh-what are we doing here? Aren't we going to get in trouble?" He tried to smooth the tremor from his voice, but doubted that he had succeeded.

"We're just catching gophers," Peaches said.

Jody blinked at him in disbelief. That's what gofering was? Weird.

"See that water spigot over there?" Peaches pointed across a narrow paved road, then nodded at the watering can. "Go fill 'er up, will ya?"

Jody hesitated, not understanding what water had to do with catching gophers or why he'd even want to help. Gophers weren't exactly good pet material—not with their sharp digging claws. Besides, they might have rabies. But everyone was looking at him, *counting* on him to do his part.

"Don't be afraid," Billy said. "T.J. always wears gloves and he's never got bit yet."

"Who's afraid?" Jody seized the watering can and went to fill it, scowling all the way. The icy water came in fits and starts, as if it had been frozen, as if it, like the robin, was making its first appearance of spring. By the time he returned, the three boys had gathered beside M–23, the number on Addison Gatley's marker, and were waiting expectantly beside an uncovered hole.

Maybe for the gopher, Jody thought. Or maybe for him. It was hard to tell.

Peaches took the can from him and started pouring water into the animal's burrow. T.J. put the gloves on, uncovered the mayonnaise jar, and inverted it over the hole.

"You're going to drown him!" Panic nipped at Jody's stomach. "Don't *do* that!"

T.J. rolled his eyes, plainly exasperated. "We're not either gonna drown him. Don't you know anything about *anything*?"

Somehow his scorn stung more than any other kid's would have. Jody bit his lip and hugged himself, unable to utter even a word in his own defense. It was hard, sometimes, he realized, to just blow off T.J.'s words. They couldn't be dismissed as having come from some kid whose opinion didn't matter.

"Don't just stand there," T.J. said. "We need more water."

For a fleeting instant, Jody considered chucking the can at T.J. and telling him to get his *own* water. But everyone was staring at him, waiting, wondering why he was such a jerk. Their unbridled contempt weakened his impulse. Maybe he was overreacting.

"It's okay." Billy, who had been kneeling beside the jar, stood up and grabbed the watering can from Jody. "*I'll* be water boy." His gaze connected for an instant with Jody's, and there was something soft and sad in his eyes. "I'm used to it," he muttered, and headed for the faucet.

A strange, melting kind of feeling pooled somewhere in Jody's chest as he watched Billy keep fetching water without complaint. Why did it have to be *T.J.* who grew up to be his father, he wondered, when Billy was so much more likable?

After each whoosh of water down the hole, T.J. and Peaches knelt around the jar, their faces flushed and eager. Jody inched closer, his curiosity finally winning out. He only hoped that T.J. had been truthful about not hurting the gopher. Maybe it *would* be exciting to see the little animal pop up into the jar, he thought.

"Won't be long now," T.J. said.

Jody eased down beside T.J., across from Peaches and Billy. The muddy ground squooshed beneath him. A chill seeped through his jeans. A mothlike fluttering tickled his stomach. He realized that he was grinning, and for no reason at all.

"I can hear him squeaking! Here he comes!" Billy pointed. "T.J., get the lid!"

Jody leaned closer to the jar as T.J. scrambled into action. A dark, wet head appeared in the glass. Tiny, scared eyes met Jody's for an instant, then darted away. We did it! his mind screamed. We really did it!

All in one motion, T.J. slid the glass from the burrow's opening and clapped the lid on behind the gopher.

"Hey, don't! You're gonna—" Jody was about to say *smother*, when he noticed that the lid had already been punched with air holes. "Sorry. Never mind."

T.J. slapped a gloved hand on Jody's back then and

pulled him into their little circle. "Ever seen one of these guys close up?" He offered the jar to Jody. "Isn't he great?"

Jody held the captured gopher and studied it with awe. The jar seemed to magnify its features—the chubby little cheeks, the chopped-off-looking tail. What a wonder that such a tiny animal could tunnel a whole maze among the tombstones! "He's great, all right," Jody said.

That unfamiliar fluttery feeling rose higher, clear up into his chest, as he passed the jar to Billy and Peaches and T.J. in turn. Finally T.J. unscrewed the cap. The gopher dove for its hole.

T.J. and Peaches clapped their hands and cheered. "Go, gopher, go! Go, gopher, go!"

Billy joined in the chorus. But Jody, worried about all the noise, glanced about the cemetery. Seeing no none, he added a whoop of his own.

T.J. raised a single eyebrow. "What's this? A little enthusiasm?"

"You ain't seen nothin' yet," Jody said, copying some TV character's line. "Get a load of this!" He raised his hand, expecting the others to follow suit and slap palms. Instead, they answered only with confused grins. "Don't you know about high-fives?" He tried to demonstrate on T.J., but for all his talk about having the best ideas, T.J. still had a lot to learn.

Chapter 10

◉ When Jody's watch sounded at 73:00, he told T.J. it was getting late—probably around twelve-forty-five.

"Oh, cripes!" T.J. looked panicked as he gathered up the watering can, gloves, and jar. "See you, Peaches. Come on!" Red-cheeked and quickly winded, he led the race for home. A monster of a car, tan-on-beige with enormous tail fins, sat in the Andersons' driveway. "Uh-oh," T.J. said. "Dad's here. You two hush up and let me do the talking."

Jody wondered what T.J. was most worried about—how late they were, their muddy clothes, or that his father had left work in the middle of the day. Maybe Mr. Anderson's headache had gotten worse. Or maybe something was wrong at his grocery store. Jody stopped in the garage to put the gophering things away. T.J., already at the back door, hissed for him to hurry up.

Billy seemed stuck to his brother's side. "Teej, you think she knows where we were?" he asked. "Maybe a little bird told her again."

"Don't be stupid," T.J. said. "Birds don't talk. But I

98

know someone else who does." He glared accusingly at Billy.

"Not me, Teej. Cross my heart and hope to die."

T.J. looked unconvinced as he led them inside, reminding them once again to let him do the talking. Jody was only too happy to oblige. Now, at the thought of meeting Mr. Anderson at last, his throat went tight, choking off everything from words to spit.

Mrs. Anderson met them at the door. "You're late, boys." Though her tone came off sounding surprisingly matter-of-fact, it didn't quite disguise the flash of annoyance in her eyes. "Go wash up now, and hurry."

The three of them crowded into a closet of a bathroom off the mudroom. T.J. turned the water on full blast, then squirted the bar of soap out of his fist at Billy. Jody's laugh sounded unnaturally high and forced.

"Stop fooling around, T.J.," his brother said—louder than he needed to, Jody noticed, unless he was actually *trying* to get T.J. in trouble.

T.J. nailed him with a hard stare and bolted for the kitchen, with Jody right behind. T.J. had plastered on an expression of pure innocence, as if to say, "See, Mom? I'm right here. What's Billy whining about?"

Mrs. Anderson's gaze seemed to linger an extra long moment on the knees of T.J.'s jeans before she examined his hands.

"I washed them," he said. "If you don't believe me, check the soap. It's sopping dry. I mean, *wet*."

Mrs. Anderson cracked a half-smile, but let T.J.'s slip

of the tongue pass without comment as he hurriedly took his seat at the table.

Jody hung back, feeling suddenly shy in T.J.'s father's presence. The man had been walled behind a newspaper but now set it aside, looking at Jody instead. His eyes, deep set and flame blue, were startlingly familiar. Jody recognized them at once as his own. The little hair Mr. Anderson had was shaved close about his ears. "So you're Jody Andrews," he said, rising and extending his hand.

At the prospect of actually touching his grandfather, who had never even been a memory, Jody's own hand went icy as a corpse's. Still, he forced it forward, all the while willing his eyes to meet Mr. Anderson's. But they rebelled, feeling at once hot and itchy, and, suddenly, his nose was running, too.

"Are you all right, son?"

Jody blinked the man into focus. Two veins throbbed in Mr. Anderson's forehead, forming that strange V that Jody had only recently noticed on his own father's forehead. He wondered fleetingly whether he, too, would someday bear the same mark. "Yes, I-I'm fine," he managed, though the strange, raspy catch in his voice brought a frown from T.J. "Are *you* feeling better, sir?"

"Some."

"That's good." Jody realized he was playing with his fingers in an annoying way that made him think of Grandma—not the one here in the past, the one who lived at the nursing home. "Thank you for letting me stay. Stay *overnight*, I mean."

"Sounds like you're in a pretty pickle," Mr. Anderson said. "Maybe we can help." He gestured for Jody to sit next to him and nudged the newspaper aside.

Help how? Not by calling child welfare, I hope. Jody glanced at the bowl of hearty vegetable-beef soup that awaited him—along with a now rubbery-looking grilled cheese sandwich. He tried to calm himself enough to eat. But his stomach clenched up like a fist.

T.J. elbowed Jody's arm. "Hamburger soup," he said. "Go on, try it. It's good."

Billy had slipped into his own seat without attracting attention. But now, his eyes trained on his bowl, he made a big show of slurping the soup. Sally's place was empty, though a milk ring by a sixth place setting hinted that she'd already eaten and gone.

Jody picked up his spoon and hesitated. Why didn't anyone ask Tom Senior why he was home so early? Mrs. Anderson placed a bowl of applesauce on the table and sat down, finally, between T.J. and Billy. She smiled almost shyly at Jody, as if encouraging him to eat, to feel at home. Somehow he managed to struggle through a first mouthful. It wasn't bad, really, and eating meant that he didn't have to talk and maybe let something slip.

"We're sorry we're late, Ma. I've been telling you I need a watch, haven't I? Jody's is busted and Peaches forgot his and—"

"You were playing at the cemetery again, weren't you," his mother said. A statement, not a question.

101

"Didn't I say no more catching gophers? Didn't I make that clear?"

Billy ate double-time.

"You said don't get into trouble, and we didn't," T.J. argued. "Nobody saw us. Heck, nobody was even there. And we didn't hurt anything."

His mother blew out a long breath as, across the table, she and her husband exchanged a pained look. "You said you were going to the park, that you were going to play ball. Do I have to say 'no catching gophers' every time you leave the house?" Leaning past T.J., she added to Jody, "I'm sorry. I just don't know what gets into him sometimes."

Jody had the strangest feeling that it wasn't just sometimes. From what he'd seen of T.J., he realized already that Dad hadn't quite told the truth about what a perfect kid he was.

"Apologize to your mother," Tom Senior said.

T.J.'s lips twitched to one side. "I'm sorry. I won't do it again." He paused, glared over at Billy, then turned to his mother. "How'd you know, anyway? How do you *always* know?"

"A little bird told me." Mrs. Anderson grinned a secret kind of smile.

"That's what you always say." T.J. sighed, clearly frustrated with her explanation.

She let the subject drop then, and Jody felt T.J. relax. Sally's words popped into his head: *Her precious little T.J.* Did Mrs. Anderson really have a soft spot for him, or was she only being nice on account of Jody's being company?

"See?" Billy said, his mouth full. "I tol' ja."

"Enough," Tom Senior said. "Can we put this behind us now and move on?" Billy, T.J., and their mother nodded in unison. "Then it's time for News Flash," he said.

T.J. set his spoon down, his face expectant. Whatever Mr. Anderson was up to, Jody thought, everybody knew about it but him.

"Want me to go get Sally?" Billy asked.

"That's all right. We'll let her off just this once." Mr. Anderson smiled and rubbed his hands together like some game show host eager to stump his guest panel. "Okay, first question." He drummed on the table. "Who is Nikita Khrushchev?"

Billy slapped his hand down an instant before T.J. did. "The president of Russia," he said, flashing a missing-toothed grin in his brother's direction.

"Premier. Close enough." Mr. Anderson slid a dime across the plastic cloth-covered surface. "Who's moving to California next week?" He pursed his lips as if trying to contain the answer.

"Don't tell me, don't tell me," T.J. said. He looked to Jody to see whether he knew, but Jody could only shrug.

"Even I don't know that one, Flash," Mrs. Anderson teased. "Give them a hint."

Mr. Anderson clapped his hands together with obvious glee. The gesture reminded Jody of his own father's delight in playing Spymaster again. "Okay, here it is: It's not just one person. Think many, think two."

"*Fla*-ash!" Mrs. Anderson laughed at the frustration on her sons' faces.

Jody bet that he looked as out of it as he felt. What a strange game! Apparently, Mr. Anderson came home for lunch *every* day; the only thing out of the ordinary today was Jody himself.

"Clue number two," Tom Senior said. "Think sports. What's the matter with you boys? You've got to read the paper. How else are you going to know what's going on in the world?"

Watch CNN? Jody wondered what Mr. Anderson would think about a twenty-four-hour news channel. Would he live long enough to know that T.J. himself grew up to be a newspaper reporter?

T.J. slapped the table so hard that the spoons jumped. "Got it! The Giants and the Dodgers, right? They're moving from New York, aren't they?" His father nodded and passed T.J. a dime. "One down, eight million to go," T.J. muttered.

No doubt he was thinking about that expensive TV repair he had to pay for. Ten cents. Big whoop. At this rate, T.J. would spend his entire childhood without television. What was Jody's two weeks compared to that? He wondered vaguely whether this time in the past would count toward their bet, or whether he'd have to start all over again once he got back. *If* he got back. He shook his head, rejecting any other possibility. It was unthinkable.

The telephone rang then, and Mr. Anderson jumped

up to answer it as if he'd been expecting a call.

"Well?" T.J. turned to his mother, keeping his voice low. "Did you already ask him? Did he say Jody could stay?"

Jody squirmed, wishing he were somewhere else. He didn't want to put her on the spot. And he didn't want to seem too eager to hear her reply. Spooning up his soup with renewed interest, he avoided her eyes. What would he do if Mr. Anderson said no?

"Ma," T.J. persisted. But his mother merely waved the question away and smiled at her husband, who was returning to the table.

"I'm sorry to have to eat and run," he said, "but Myron's wife is having her baby. He's meeting her at the hospital, so I'm needed behind the meat counter."

"But what about Jody?" T.J. blurted. "Can he stay?"

"Uh . . ." Mr. Anderson was patting his pockets down in a most distracted way.

"Please? We promise no more gophers."

"Sure. Fine."

"Oh, goody!" Billy clasped his hands beneath his chin and beamed at Jody. "I'm gonna go tell Sally we've got a new foster kid."

Jody's jaw sagged open in surprise. That wasn't what Mr. Anderson had intended. Wasn't even what T.J. had meant—had he? It was impossible to tell from that impish grin still plastered on his face. Surely Mrs. Anderson didn't want another kid around all the time. She already had three times more laundry and cooking and mess than Jody's own mother had. On the other hand, it *was* the olden days, and Mrs. Anderson was able to stay at home and not go to work.

Jody tried to make sense of her reaction to Billy's announcement—that secret smile again and a silence that for some reason made the hair on his arms bristle. Why was she looking at him so intently? Did she know something that he didn't—or, even worse, that she *shouldn't*?

"Thanks, Dad," T.J. said, and jumped from his chair to hug his father. "You won't regret it."

"Regret what?" Mr. Anderson pulled a set of keys from his vest pocket and waved them triumphantly.

T.J. clucked his tongue. "Jody staying. What have we been talking about?"

"Please, sir, I won't be any trouble." The words, the slight pleading tone in his own voice, amazed Jody. He had no intention of staying any longer than he needed to.

Tom Senior rubbed his balding head in a way that made Jody realize that he was only now considering T.J.'s question.

"Come on, Dad. It's vacation, no school, remember? Just let him *visit*, then. Don't be a meanie," T.J. said.

Mr. Anderson worked his jaw for a long moment. Unspoken pleas seemed to come from every corner of the table—from T.J. and Billy, and even from their mother. "Well . . . ," Mr. Anderson said at last, "all right. But only until after our anniversary, you hear me,

Claire? And then we really *should* call child welfare."

T.J.'s mother nodded, looked down for several moments, then abruptly bounced up and circled around to peck him on the cheek. He wagged his finger at her in a way that Jody didn't understand. But Mrs. Anderson only laughed off the scolding and began bustling about the kitchen.

"When's their anniversary?" Jody whispered to T.J.

"Search me. But I think we'd better find out. Quick." T.J. spooned up the last of his soup. "Come on. Let's go ask Sally. Fingers crossed she's in a good mood."

Chapter 11

From the doorway, Jody spied Sally's underwear, all piled up on her dresser. His brakes went on. He could follow T.J. and Billy no further—at least, not without being invited. Not that he really *wanted* to be. Even from here, Sally's bedroom gave him the creeps. He'd never seen so much purple in one place. It was like having faded grape jelly smeared from carpet to ceiling. The only break was a giant Elvis poster on the wall next to Sally's bed—and even the mattress seemed to float on a pile of purple ruffles.

The poster was of *young* Elvis, Jody noted, vaguely remembering a post office vote between two different stamp designs. *Fat* Elvis was what everyone called the other one. Jody smiled at the memory. He could still hear Mom going on about how unfair that was, how people should have called it *Older* Elvis instead. He'd have to remember to call Aunt Sally in Oregon once he got back home and ask what she had called that stamp design.

"So, are you going to tell us or not?" T.J. was saying.

Sally chewed on the end of her ponytail, toying with

her brothers. "Why should I tell you guys?" she said at last. "It's not like you ever get them a present or anything."

"Well . . ." T.J. looked over his shoulder at Jody, probably debating whether to tell her the real reason for their interest. "Maybe we will this year."

"Yeah, maybe we will," Billy chimed in.

Sally unwrapped a piece of bubble gum and popped it into her mouth. Just *tell* us already, Jody thought. How many more days before they send me away?

She worked the gum without speaking for a long moment, then almost smirked at T.J. "Like you're really rolling in money, right?"

T.J. stuffed his hands into his pockets, his eyes downcast. Jody suddenly wished that he hadn't spent all of his last week's allowance on movie rentals. If only it were still in *his* pocket, he'd give the whole five dollars to T.J. That would cheer him up.

"I could make 'em a card," Billy said, "if you just say when it is." Mustering a pitiful face that he'd most likely learned from T.J., he drew closer to his sister.

She rumpled his hair, as much as porcupine hair would rumple. "It's the day after tomorrow."

So soon? What if Jody couldn't figure out how to get back by then? Two days was, what? Forty-eight hours? As his brain whizzed through the math, Jody's pulse quickened. At this time on the Andersons' anniversary day, he realized, his watch would read 24:30—leaving one full day plus a half an hour in its relentless countdown. *Until what?* He couldn't imagine what awaited him at 00:00.

Sally popped her gum smugly, managing to avoid a pink mess on her nose and cheeks. "I already know what *I'm* going to get them."

"Yeah?" T.J. said. "What?" He and Billy leaned toward their sister as if they expected her to whisper her reply.

As if, Jody thought, still listening from the doorway, the three of them were all on the same team. A sudden stab of loneliness both confused and surprised him. What had he expected? That they were going to treat him like a new brother or something?

"Dinner for two at Chez Louis." She pronounced it *Shay LooEE*—Jody supposed it was some fancy French place—and folded her arms across her chest as if to say "Top that."

"Ha! And double ha!" T.J. said. "Don't make me laugh. You couldn't afford *one* dinner at Chez Louis. Matter of fact, you couldn't afford a glass of milk at Chez Louis."

"What do *you* know, anyway?" Sally chewed at a hang-nail and looked away. "Go on," she said, "just get out of here. Both of you." She glared at Jody. "*All* of you."

Billy shuffled glumly toward the doorway. T.J., however, made no move to go. He was biting on his bottom lip and nodding his head—about what, Jody had no idea. At last he snapped his fingers.

"I said *go*." Sally, taller and heavier, tried to bully T.J. toward the door.

"Just hear me out. I've got an idea. A *great* idea."

"I'll bet."

"Really. And it won't cost us hardly anything."

Sally raised one eyebrow. T.J. needed no more encouragement to motion Jody and Billy into the room. Despite Sally's protests, T.J. closed her door behind them.

"We can make 'em dinner ourselves." T.J.'s eyes shone. "Make it real fancy and dress up like waiters, just like at Chez Louis."

"That wouldn't work," Sally said.

"Why not?" Jody blurted. The others looked as astonished to hear his voice as he felt to have spoken. He wasn't part of this, not really. Why was he getting so caught up in it?

"Yeah," Billy chimed in, "why not?"

"Because we can't cook, that's why," Sally said.

"All we've got to do is follow a recipe." T.J. rolled his eyes in exasperation.

"Yeah," Jody said, "and if worse comes to worst, we can just nuke something in the microwave."

"The *what*?" Sally and Billy spoke in unison. T.J. shook his head as if to say "Not this future stuff again."

"The . . . uh . . . never mind. It was just a joke." Strike two, Jody thought. Me and my big mouth.

T.J. slapped Jody on the back. "He's such a kidder. You've got to know how to take him."

Sally snapped her gum. "Well, *you* can take him out of here."

"No, really," T.J. said, "couldn't we send them an invitation? Couldn't we call the store and have Lenny deliver what we need and charge it to Dad?"

Sally sighed. "I guess so." She flopped down on her bed and gazed dreamily up at the Elvis poster. "But we need to make it romantic. You know, like in the movies."

"Yuck," Billy said.

T.J. shot his brother a warning look. "You're right," he said to Sally. "You're absolutely right. Why don't you be in charge of the mushy stuff and me and Jody will be in charge of the food."

"What am I in charge of?" Billy asked.

"Table setting," T.J. replied. "Matter of fact, you can be in charge of all the waiters."

"Me? All by myself? Oh, goody!" Billy danced in place. "Goody, goody gumdrops!"

"So," T.J. said, "is it a plan? Me and Jody'll go make the invitation, okay?"

"Okay, already." Sally sounded annoyed, but Jody noticed that the corners of her mouth were turning up ever so slightly. "Go on, and I'll pick out the perfect menu."

T.J. hurried the other boys out of her room. "This is supposed to be a surprise," he said to Billy, "so keep your yap shut, you hear?" Billy nodded solemnly. "You wait in my room," T.J. said. "We'll go get the art box."

"I wanna come, too." Billy pouted.

"I *said*, wait here." T.J. turned to Jody, dismissing his brother. "Come on."

Jody blinked at T.J., words piling up at the back of his throat. Why couldn't he say something? What a wimp he was, not sticking up for Billy, following T.J. downstairs like some meek little puppy. As they went past the living room, he couldn't resist glancing at the TV, at the dark void above the control panel. What shows would they be watching if it weren't broken? Did they even have good cartoons in the olden days?

From the kitchen came the sound of T.J.'s parents' strained voices. "I told you I've got to go. I'm late. Let's just drop this, Claire," Mr. Anderson was saying. "It can't happen. We don't know anything about him."

Who are they talking about? Me? Jody's fingers felt suddenly itchy and nervous, the way they often did around the remote control. He didn't want to listen. Look at the conclusion he'd jumped to last time.

T.J. waved him up against the wall, his finger to his lips.

"He's special. Can't you *feel* how special he is? It's like we're connected somehow. I can't explain it."

"Of course he's special. Every child is. But that doesn't mean—"

"Oh, please, Flash," she said. "Just think about it. He belongs here. I can feel it in my bones."

Mr. Anderson cleared his throat. "Just like you feel the weather changing, is that it?"

"Have you looked into his eyes, dear? I mean, *really* looked?"

T.J. whirled on Jody, a strange expression contorting

his face. Jody's stomach rose and fell in a heartbeat. Without quite knowing why, he began backing away from T.J., from the kid who would grow up to be his own father. He'd heard enough. Maybe too much. They both had.

"Where do you think *you're* going?" T.J. said, his voice low. "This is just getting interesting."

"We . . . we shouldn't be listening."

"Maybe not. But they shouldn't be talking about you behind your back, should they?" T.J. caught Jody's wrist. "Come on back here."

Jody wished he could make himself pull away. But T.J.'s grasp seemed to have the strength of a forty-something-year-old man's. Now Jody's legs turned to jelly. It must be true then; even T.J. thought so. They *were* talking about him. This time Jody hadn't jumped to conclusions or let his imagination run wild. "I-I don't understand," he stammered. "What's the big—"

"Shhh!" T.J. pressed himself against the dark paneling in the hall outside the kitchen.

A chair scritched across the linoleum. "I've got to get back to work," Mr. Anderson said. "We can talk about this later."

"Yes. We can."

"Come on, Claire. Cheer up, please? Let's look forward to our big day. I've even figured out what I'm going to get you."

"Really?" She sounded as excited as a little kid. "You're not going to make me wait, are you?"

Mr. Anderson laughed. "Better not. You just might go off and spend all your Green Stamps on a new one."

"On what? Tell me."

"A new TV. I've called the repairman. He'll be here Thursday."

T.J. stifled a cheer, but Jody stiffened at the news. That TV—minus its screen—might be his only way to get home again. What would happen if it were fixed?

"That's wonderful!" T.J.'s mother said. "I'll get to watch my ballet, then."

"Yes, and Sally can watch her precious Ed Sullivan."

"What about T.J.? Surely you're not letting him—"

"Definitely not," Mr. Anderson said. "He'll pay me back, every last cent, before he ever watches TV again. You mark my words."

T.J. glowered at Jody as if everything were his fault. "Where did you come from, really?" he demanded. "What're you doing here?"

"I-I don't know. I already told you." Jody tried to swallow the rising lump in his throat.

"Ha! And double ha!" T.J. blinked quickly. "You came to make trouble for me, didn't you? Tell the truth."

"I *am* telling the truth," Jody said. "Swear to God." He squirmed under T.J.'s dark gaze. It felt as if the kid were boring holes through his skull.

"Then what's the deal with you and my mom?" T.J. asked, peering hard into Jody's eyes. "What makes *you* so special?"

Chapter 12

⊚ "T.J.!" Jody's cheeks went hot with frustration. "Like I told you before, I don't understand *any* of this."

T.J. appeared to chew on the inside of one cheek, working the silence.

Jody squirmed. Should he admit who he *really* was? Chances were, T.J. wouldn't believe it. And even if he did, was it worth the risk? T.J. might do something on purpose to change the future. What if he wasn't satisfied with Jody as a son and decided to marry someone else? In that case, there might be no Jody at all!

The very thought set his stomach to churning. How could he not *be*, not exist anywhere at all, if he was here, now? He steadied himself against the wall—something solid, something he could count on.

"I'm still waiting for an explanation," T.J. said, but folded his arms across his chest as if to deflect anything he didn't want to hear.

"Look, I already told you how I got here and you don't believe me. What do you want me to say? I don't know your mom. *You* do." All Jody knew was that she was crazy in the future. Maybe she was starting to go crazy now. His heart was hammering in his ears. He struggled to keep his voice low. "Maybe . . . maybe I should just go."

"Go? Go where?"

Jody shrugged. "I don't know. Somewhere."

"You'd leave? Really?"

Even if he knew *how* to get home again, Jody didn't really want to. Not until after the anniversary dinner. But there was no point now in staying around any longer if he wasn't welcome. "I'd go if you wanted me to," Jody said. "Of course I would."

"Just like that?" T.J. frowned. "You mean, all I have to do is ask and you'd disappear, never to be heard of again?"

Jody smirked, hiding the truth. "You could say that. Yeah."

"So, you're not here to make trouble, right?"

"Honest. That's the last thing I'd want to do."

Time seemed to stop for an instant as T.J. searched Jody's eyes. "Oh, never mind," he said abruptly. "You don't have to go. I mean, who *cares* where you came from? You're here, right? Look. Maybe you *could* be another foster kid—one that *I* like, for a change. So don't go, okay? Promise?"

Jody fidgeted, confused by T.J.'s sudden turnabout. What was he supposed to say to a kid whose moods blew hot and cold and changed as fast as Wisconsin weather? He *wanted* to say he liked T.J. He really did. But he'd be stretching the truth. It was Billy he felt closer to. Still, it would be no lie to say he wanted to keep trying. For all T.J.'s talk about having friends and the best ideas, there was something almost desperate and lonely about him. Something, Jody realized with a start, that he himself understood.

"Come on, Jody. Just promise, will you? I don't want you to go. I was only kidding. Really. We'll have fun. You'll see."

It was strange, hearing T.J. beg. If only he knew how ridiculous that was—a father begging his son! It was a relief, though. A gift of more time. "Okay," Jody said, "I'll stay as long as I can." His watch beeped then, reminding him that time was, indeed, something *not* to be wasted.

"Great!" T.J. clapped Jody on the back. "Let's go make that invitation, then."

As they entered the kitchen, Mr. Anderson was kissing Mrs. Anderson good-bye. Jody hung back, embarrassed. He felt that way around his own parents sometimes, but this was different. This time he wasn't the only outsider looking on; his father was a kid, too.

"It's all right." Mrs. Anderson laughed. "Don't mind us."

Jody hurried after T.J., who had begun rummaging through a deep drawer in the dining area.

"What are you boys up to this afternoon?" Tom Senior asked. "Not monkey business, I hope."

"No, sir," Jody said. "And not gopher business either."

T.J.'s father smiled as he buttoned his sweater. "Just what T.J. needs. A good influence."

Mrs. Anderson nodded as if to say "I told you so."

Her husband sent a silent reply with his eyes that Jody did not understand. After asking her whether she needed anything from the store, Mr. Anderson said he'd see everyone at supper and rushed off.

T.J., meanwhile, had found some construction paper and colored pencils. He motioned Jody to follow him.

"What're you making?" his mother asked, not turning from the dishes she was rinsing and setting on a wire draining rack. Jody wondered whether she had eyes in the back of her head the way his own mother seemed to.

"Making? Oh . . . nothing," T.J. said. He hissed for Jody to hurry.

But Jody was guiltily eyeing several dirty dishes that remained on the table. His own. Raising a finger, he signaled T.J. to wait while he ferried them to the sink.

Mrs. Anderson beamed. "What a dear boy! Thank you!"

Uncomfortable with the praise, Jody hung his head. Out of the corner of his eye, he caught T.J. mimicking his mother in the hallway, then glaring at him anew. Now what? Jody wondered. Thrusting his hand into his pocket, he fingered his watch, remembering his *real* life. There, T.J. was the grown-up father he longed to spend more time with, not this moody kid whose hard gaze made his knees go weak. "Well," Jody said to Mrs. Anderson, backing toward the door, "if that's all . . ."

She winked. "That's plenty. You boys run along. Supper's at six."

T.J.'s expression slipped back into neutral as Jody approached. "Come on." He raced for the stairs and Jody clattered after him. "You're such a kissy-face," T.J. said, closing his door.

"What's wrong with that? I thought you wanted her to like me, to let me stay."

"I do. Only . . . never mind."

Jody debated whether to press him further. If he really wanted to know his father better, here was his chance. Still, Jody's pulse raced at the thought of poking around too much in T.J.'s life and setting him off again. Maybe some things were better not known. . . .

"What?" T.J. demanded. "Why are you looking at me that way?"

"What way?"

"Like a doctor or something. Cut it out, will you? It gives me the creeps."

Jody simply nodded, and T.J. spread the colored paper on his desk, pulled out a pair of scissors, and set to work designing the invitation. Where had Billy gone? Jody wondered. Wasn't he supposed to wait here and help, too? Something told him not to ask.

After several botched attempts at writing *You are cordially invited*, T.J. turned to Jody. "How's your printing?"

"It's okay." Jody didn't want to brag. The truth was, his handwriting was better than most girls'—even if he *did* hold his pen the wrong way. It was funny to realize, though, that his father's handwriting hadn't improved much over the years. Dad always said he liked telephone interviews for just that reason—he could take notes on his computer and not have to worry about later deciphering his own handwritten ones. "I'll do it if you want me to," Jody offered.

T.J. dictated and Jody wrote:

You are cordially invited
to a special anniversary dinner
Wednesday evening at 6 p.m.
at Chez Anderson

"That looks too plain," T.J. said. "We need to add something."

"How about a candle or a flower or . . . ?"

T.J. chewed on his lip. At last he grabbed the scissors, cut a strip of red paper, and curled it around a pencil. "One rosebud coming right up," he said, scooping up a glob of thick white paste that smelled like root beer. T.J. seemed to enjoy playing with the stuff as much as using it to glue the rosebud down. When he was finally finished, he sucked his fingers in turn.

Jody drew his face up in disgust.

"It tastes *good*," T.J. said. "You ought to try it."

Jody shuddered at the very idea. "No, thanks."

T.J. stood up abruptly and swept his scraps into an already messy desk drawer. "Let's go get Billy and Sally to sign this," he said. "We'll give it to Mom and Dad at supper."

Jody tagged after T.J. as he went from Billy's room to Sally's, where they found the others.

Sally scanned the invitation with grudging admiration and turned to Jody. "Did you do this writing?" When he nodded, she added, "I figured it wasn't Pigpen here."

T.J. punched her shoulder; she slapped him back. Jody couldn't tell whether they were teasing or serious. Billy, however, darted out of the way as if he knew, from experience, not to get caught in the middle.

"Come on, T.J.," Jody said. "Let's go do something." What, he had no idea. But one good thing about T.J., he was bound to have enough ideas for the both of them.

Sticking his tongue out at his sister, T.J. retrieved the card from Sally's desk and started for the door. Jody headed out, too, but Billy plucked him back by the shirt. "Aren't *you* going to sign it? You helped, too."

"I, uh . . ." Jody faltered. Sally's arms were folded across her chest. Her chin angled upward as if defying him to say yes. T.J., on the other hand, was nodding enthusiastically.

"Of course he's going to sign it," T.J. said. "He wrote it, didn't he? He's helping with the cooking and stuff."

"Oh, all right." With a great sigh, she turned to Billy. "Go swipe Mom's cookbook—will you?—and bring it to me."

Billy rolled his eyes. "Why do I always have to go for everything?"

"'Cause you're the gofer," T.J. said. "Get it?" He elbowed his little brother in the ribs. Jody bit back a grin, picturing a miniature Billy shut up in a jar with holes in its lid.

"Not funny." Billy stuck his lip out, working the pout for all it was worth. Jody made a mental note to try that sometime on his father once he got home. He wondered whether Dad would recognize the routine.

"Pretty please with a cherry on top?" Sally batted her eyelashes at Billy. "I'll let you help me plan the dinner."

"Okay. I'll get it." Billy trudged off, sulking.

T.J. motioned Jody into his room and thrust the card at him. "Go on. Sign it."

Jody hesitated. "You really want me to?"

"Sure. Why not? Anything to make Mom happy."

Jody wished he could tell from T.J.'s tone whether he was being sincere or sarcastic. Either way, he suddenly realized, he wanted to be a part of this anniversary gift. He tried to imagine his own parents' reaction if he were to pull off a surprise like this. But he doubted that he could do it—or that it would be much fun—alone.

T.J. nudged his arm. "Well, hurry up and sign, would ya?" He grabbed a couple of sweatshirts off the bed and tossed one to Jody. "The guys'll be waiting for us down at the park. You wanna be third base? I've got an extra mitt. Or how about outfield . . . ?"

T.J.'s chatter reminded Jody of Saturday morning cartoons, familiar now and somehow comforting. It filled the room, demanding nothing from him, as he bent over the desk and neatly penned his first name near the bottom, just to the left of where T.J. had written *love*.

Chapter 13

◎ The rest of the day whirred by, with each beep of Jody's watch seeming to come faster than the last. At the park, T.J.'s friends hadn't cared *where* Jody had come from—only that he was willing to play right field and be last up to bat. He supposed someone had to, and it wasn't as if he were a great player.

At last came suppertime, and the moment Jody and the others had been waiting for all day. Accompanied by a fanfare of table-drumming, Billy presented the anniversary invitation on a red velvet pillow. "Flash, isn't this something?" Mrs. Anderson said. "I can hardly wait till tomorrow night!" You and me both, Jody thought.

Lying in his sleeping bag, though, he began to worry how few hours would be left on his watch by dinnertime Wednesday. Nineteen, if his math was correct. The relentless countdown made his stomach knot. What did it all mean?

T.J.'s breathing, even and slow, came from across the room. Jody wished he could sleep, too, if only to stop his thoughts from spinning like cyclones in the dark. Mrs. Anderson's quick good-night hadn't helped calm him—

not like reading with Mom would have, although he'd never admit that to T.J. "Only Billy still has bedtime stories," T.J. would probably say. He was just the type to think that, at almost twelve, he and Jody were way too old for them.

Scrunching his pillow into a ball, Jody closed his eyes and tried to picture what his parents were doing right now without him. He'd been gone much longer than a day, or so it seemed. Did they think he'd run away—or been kidnapped? Were the police out looking for him? Questions buzzed through his brain like pesky gnats. He couldn't shake them *or* the fear that, after last night's failed attempt, he might never get home at all. If only this were some scary TV movie he could turn off at will!

At last, restless, Jody stole downstairs and sat cross-legged in front of the broken television. He stared at the strange, grinning control panel. Too bad the TV set couldn't do the outrageous and speak. Surely it would know the secret, the key to going home.

"You miss TV, too, huh?"

Jody spun about to see Billy standing behind him. "That's not all I miss," he said softly.

Billy hunkered down beside him. The streetlight through the partially drawn drapes cast a ghostly pallor across the boy's face. "Don't you like it here?'

"Sure I do," Jody replied. "It's just that . . ." Was Billy really the blabbermouth T.J. said he was?

"You wanna go home, huh?"

Jody nodded. "I just wish I knew how."

Billy patted Jody's arm and said nothing. But the way he just sat there, silent and trusting, seemed to nag at Jody until the next thing he knew, he was blurting out everything. Well, *almost* everything. He didn't tell Billy that T.J. and Dad were the same person, but he did jabber on about playing Spymaster with him, climbing into the TV, and zapping back in time. And though he had no idea why, he even told Billy about the strange beeping countdown on his watch.

Billy's eyes went wide as an owl's in the near darkness. "Wow, really? What happens when it gets to zero?"

"I wish I knew."

"I wanna go in there. Can you zap me, too?"

Jody shook his head. "I don't know how to make it work again."

"Maybe it's part of the game." Billy yawned. "You're not playing right."

"Playing *what* right—Spymaster?"

"I don't know. Maybe."

Jody suddenly felt like shaking the kid until every thing he did know came spilling out. "Play with me, Billy, okay?"

"Right now?" Billy yawned again. "That's crazy. I can't. I've gotta go back to bed."

"No! Please! You can even be Spymaster, all right?" He *did* sound crazy. No wonder Billy was backing away from him, shaking his head. "Please, Bill? Even if you find me, I won't demote you, okay? And next time—"

"There won't *be* a next time," Billy said quietly, "if you go."

Smart kid. Jody dug his bare toes into the nubby carpet, hunching his shoulders against the draft that played through the room. He didn't know what to say, how to explain the sudden desperation he felt.

"Okay," Billy said at last, and sighed. "I'll do it." He ambled sleepily to the bottom of the stairs, hid his eyes, and began counting in a harsh whisper.

Jody darted for the TV set, his pulse racing. This had to work. It just *had* to. He quickly climbed inside and peered at his glowing watch face. Though the seconds seemed to drag, he could see that they were indeed ticking steadily downward. Jody's own heartbeat competed with the sound of Billy's counting. He squinched his eyes shut, waiting, hoping. Moments later, he felt someone tapping on his leg.

"Mom?" Jody craned to see who was there. "Dad?"

Billy's face appeared in the opening. A clunk registered in the pit of Jody's stomach. "Only me," the boy said. "Sorry."

Jody bit back the swear word he wanted to say and climbed out. Why didn't it work? He'd been sure that Billy was onto something. Now, the poor kid looked so disappointed, as if he'd personally made the time travel fail, that Jody reached out and ruffled his hair. "Well, it was worth a try. Thanks, anyway. You want me to be Spymaster now?"

Billy stifled another yawn and shook his head. "I wanna go back to bed, okay?"

Jody supposed he ought to as well. Maybe tomorrow he'd figure things out. He'd better. From the numbers on his watch—59:45—he knew he was running out of time.

The next thing Jody knew, sunshine washed over his face. He opened his eyes, squinting against the glare. T.J.'s bed was already made—if you could call it that—the brown corduroy spread thrown willy-nilly over the covers.

Jody blinked at T.J.'s Woody Woodpecker clock, unbelieving. The round face said ten-thirty. He must have slept like a dead person, that was for sure—hadn't heard the pipes gurgle when Mr. Anderson showered, hadn't heard T.J. get up, either.

Jody scrambled to wash and dress, grateful that Sally was holed up in her room, singing along with her Elvis records. The smell of bacon hung in the air, making his stomach grumble as he hurried downstairs.

"Good morning, Sleepy Head!"

Jody started at the sound of Mrs. Anderson's voice, unsure where it was coming from.

"I'm behind you, in the den."

He turned and noticed a door ajar at the base of the stairs. She was sitting in an easy chair, crocheting. Classical music played softly in the background.

"Where is everybody—T.J., I mean?"

"He and Bill are out riding bikes. I told him to let you sleep."

Jody nodded and ventured into the tiny room. A polished wood box gleamed on an end table in the lamplight. He stared at it, trying to place the vague, uneasy feeling that stole over him. Lacy circles that looked like snowflakes lay beside it. They made him think of the long crocheted strip he'd seen on Grandma's dresser in the nursing home.

"Come sit." She moved her feet to one side of the ottoman, making room for him.

"Those are pretty," Jody said. As he watched her crochet hook weave a single strand into chains, then patterns, he tried not to think about the box on the table, not to look at it, either. "What you're doing," he said, "it looks hard."

She shook her head, and blond curls bounced about her face like a schoolgirl's. "My grandmother taught me, years ago. Most other people knit. I suppose it's more practical." She shrugged apologetically. "But I like this."

Jody nodded but said nothing. His mind spun with images of her, present and future, that didn't seem to mesh—and with things he wanted to ask her, if only he could gather the courage. Things like, What was in that wooden box?

"You must be hungry," she said. "I left you some breakfast on the stove, but it's probably cold by now."

"That's okay, thanks. I can nu—uh, never mind." He swallowed the word *nuke*. What did people do without microwave ovens? With a last wistful glance toward the end table, he headed for the kitchen, unnerved that Mrs.

Anderson was following him. What did she think he was—a baby who couldn't pour his own milk? Or maybe . . . He tried to reject the very thought. It seemed impossible. But what if for some reason she didn't trust him?

Through the window over the sink he could see T.J. and Billy, riding their bicycles in the street. Something was dripping from the metal can on T.J.'s back fender. A dark line marked the pavement behind him.

"What are they doing?" Jody asked.

"With the water, you mean?" T.J.'s mother laughed. "They pretend it's gas and when the tank is empty, they can't ride until they buy some more."

Jody raised one eyebrow. Strange, he thought. T.J. was definitely strange. "They pay for water?"

"Not with money, of course. With flattened bottle caps."

Jody vaguely recalled his father's stories. "That's fun?" he blurted, and at once wished he hadn't. He didn't want Mrs. Anderson to think that he was making fun of her sons.

"Maybe you have to be there," she said. "But I can tell you, T.J.'s not one for doing things he doesn't enjoy."

Jody guessed that made sense. Maybe it was like gophering—better in the doing.

"Go have a seat." She lifted the plate that she'd used to cover his breakfast, to try to keep it warm. "I think this is still edible." She set some blueberry pancakes and bacon before him, then pulled a chair up alongside.

"Looks good to me," Jody said, and smiled appreciatively. He felt her laser-sharp gaze on him as he stuffed
an oversized piece into his mouth.

"So, what are we going to do with you, Mr. Jody . . .
Andrews, isn't it?'"

Jody nodded, eyes trained on his pancakes. What was
she getting at?

"I don't want to get your hopes up, but maybe the
child welfare people would let *us* take you in. We've had
lots of foster kids and—"

"Yeah, T.J. told me."

"You'd probably have to go with them for a couple of
days while they do the paperwork and all. But still . . ."
Her voice trailed off and she seemed to debate the
situation silently. "I'd sure hate the thought of them
sending you somewhere else, not when you fit in so well
here."

Jody hated the thought even more than she did. He
tried a bite of bacon, but it seemed to crumble and stick
in his throat. He began to cough.

"Are you all right?" She thumped him on the back.

"Fine," he managed to rasp.

"So, what would you think, about our being your
foster family, I mean? Would you like that?" When he
nodded, she hurried on. "I'm not sure how long it
would take to get things all squared away, but maybe I
could call and find out."

"No, please!" Jody's protest seemed to explode from
some dark corner of his being, from the place where fear

hid. He'd heard all about government agencies from Dad—how they took forever to get things done. If he left this house with one of *those* people, he was as good as stuck in the past forever. "Don't call. Not yet. Not until after we all celebrate your anniversary, okay?"

A strange, faraway look stole over Mrs. Anderson's face. Color seemed to flood her cheeks. "You said *we all*." She smiled at him.

Jody licked his lips, seizing his opening. His pulse quickened. "Do you think . . . you know me or something?"

Mrs. Anderson nodded, but did not explain.

"I-I heard you say that yesterday."

"Yes. I did." She hugged herself and glanced away for an instant, then locked her gaze on his. "There's something about your eyes. I don't know. It's strange, and of course Tom doesn't believe me, but . . . ." She shrugged helplessly. "You must think I'm some crazy voodoo woman."

Jody shook his head. "Heck, everybody gets *vibes* sometimes, you know? It doesn't mean you're . . . crazy." Not yet. Hopefully not ever.

"Vibes?"

"Vibrations, feelings, brain waves. You know."

"Yes, I guess I do. *Vibes.* What a wonderful word!"

Jody steeled his courage. "Where . . . where do you think you know me from?"

"Maybe from Milwaukee? We lived there when the kids were little, before Flash bought the market. I thought maybe you were in one of their play groups. Or maybe a student at my dance school?"

"I don't think so." She ran a dance school? It was hard to believe that the frail, forgetful grandmother he knew had ever done such a thing. "You're a dancer? Really?"

She nodded, smiling shyly. "Or, rather, I used to be. Never quite made it big, though. I like to think it was because I'm not *tall enough*—no joke intended."

"But that's cool, anyway. I never knew that about you. Dad never—" He broke off; his mind raced for a good cover-up. He rubbed his clammy palms on his jeans. "I mean, *T.J.'s* dad never, um, mentioned it. To me, I mean. But why would he, right?" His laugh sounded tight and tinny as he started up from the table to clear the dishes, to avoid her eyes.

But Mrs. Anderson touched his arm, detaining him for a moment. She frowned at him, then seemed to shrug off whatever thought she'd been wrestling with, and let him go.

"Well, thanks for breakfast," he said, trying to sound like his old self despite the sudden pounding in his chest. Surely she could hear his voice quaver, see his cheeks flush. "I think I'd better go catch T.J."

"Yes, dear. You do that. We'll talk again."

Beneath the words, he could sense her wistfulness and her confusion. And though he wanted to confess the truth about himself, to reassure her that she wasn't crazy for sensing a connection between them, he didn't dare turn back.

Chapter 14

◎ After supper that night, Jody, T.J., and Billy met in Sally's room to divide up the list of things to do for the anniversary dinner the next evening. She had already decided on the menu—Beef Stroganoff with noodles and salad. For dessert, they were going to serve something called Peaches Flambé. Jody hoped they could make it catch fire the way the cookbook picture showed. Never having *seen* flaming fruit before, let alone cooked it, he squirmed with excitement at the adventure they were all about to undertake together.

Sally would order the food from the market in the morning and have it delivered. T.J. and Jody would set the table and choose some music. Billy, declared head-waiter by Sally over T.J.'s objections, wanted to make menus. And everyone would help with the cooking and serving.

At bedtime, to Jody's surprise, Mrs. Anderson took his suggestion from earlier in the day and read aloud to them the first chapter of *Charlotte's Web*. Even more surprising was that T.J. kept his mouth shut and didn't say one word about being too old to be read to.

After she'd gone and they were finally in bed, T.J. said, "Jody, I can't believe how excited you are about all this anniversary stuff."

"I know. Weird, isn't it?"

"Yes. Very."

"What's that supposed to mean?" Jody wasn't quite sure whether to feel insulted or defensive.

"I don't know. You tell me. I mean, it's not like I want you to leave or anything. Don't get me wrong. It's just that . . . oh, never mind."

Jody wished he could see T.J.'s face. "No, really," he said. "I want to know."

"First promise you won't get mad."

"Why would I?"

"Just *promise*," T.J. said, and Jody did. "The thing is, this is *my* family, you know? I feel bad that you don't have your own and all, but you can't just show up and take over somebody else's."

"I-I'm not."

"Y'are, too! I see how Billy acts around you. Ma, too. They think you're so perfect, right up there with Wonder Bread."

Jody sighed. "Isn't that how you're supposed to act when you're company?"

T.J. did not reply, and in the silence, Jody's confusion snowballed. T.J. had said that he still wanted him here, but why? It seemed that Jody was always giving him something to complain about. "T.J.?" he whispered. "You still awake?"

"Yeah."

"Whatever I did . . . I'm sorry, okay?" His watch beeped then—39:00—as if it, like T.J., were chiding him for getting so wrapped up in the past and T.J.'s family. But what choice did he have? Both times he'd tried to get home, he had failed completely. For now, at least, there was nothing to do but make the best of things. "Pssst! T.J.! I said I'm *sorry*, okay?"

"Okay, already. I heard you," T.J. snapped. "Sheesh, that thing's annoying, going off every hour. Keep it in your pocket, why dontcha? Or maybe have Dad take it in to get fixed."

"No, it'll be all right." Jody couldn't say why, but somehow he knew that the watch must not leave his hands. Still, he'd have to remember not to wear it, not to let it attract attention. "Bet you won't even hear it, after a while," Jody said, making one last attempt to smooth things over between them.

T.J., however, was already deaf, asleep, or pretending to be both.

For the first time since his arrival, Jody slept through the night without awakening. In the morning, T.J. talked him into playing Mud Bowl—football in the mud— with the neighbor kids to help pass the time. Between running from house to house to assemble the teams, playing the actual game, and cleaning up afterward, Jody supposed that it was a good thing that he was so well rested.

By the time Sally shooed her mother out of the kitchen and upstairs to go dress for the anniversary dinner, the rest of the day's activities were nothing but a blur, Jody realized.

"And don't come down till we call you, Mommy," Sally hollered up at the ceiling.

As he'd deliberately done all day, Jody hung back, letting T.J. do the talking and take center stage. With the big dinner so close at hand, Jody didn't want to risk bringing on another one of the kid's moods.

"Need any help?" T.J. asked his sister.

Sally's ponytail swished as she shook her head. "Why don't you go set the table and get the music ready. I'll call you if I need you."

"Just don't let *him* mess up the menus," said T.J., inclining his head toward Billy, who was hunkered over the kitchen table with some paper and crayons.

Billy stuck out his tongue. "Mind your own beeswax," he said.

"I am." T.J. grinned.

Jody wondered whether T.J. ever got check marks on his report card for "doesn't work well with others." What a pain he'd be in a school cooperation group, always snapping orders like that, Jody thought. Not that *he'd* have the nerve to tell him off. Instead, he tugged on T.J.'s arm. "Come on. Let's get out of here."

A swinging door from the kitchen opened onto a formal dining room. Jody, surprised by the cut-crystal chandelier, fancy polished table, and cane-backed chairs, wondered whether there were other rooms he hadn't seen. It would be no problem making this place look like an expensive restaurant. All they had to do was add flowers, candles, and a good tablecloth.

T.J. fished in a drawer of the china hutch and at last pulled out two cloth napkins and lacy placemats. They looked like the kind of thing Mrs. Anderson might have crocheted. "Here," T.J. said. "Put these on the table."

"Are you *always* so bossy?" Jody couldn't believe he'd actually spoken his thoughts aloud.

T.J. started at the question. "I-I'm not . . . am I?"

"Yeah, you are. You should hear yourself."

T.J. bit his lower lip, avoiding Jody's eyes. Silently, he retrieved two settings of silverware from a wooden chest, a larger version, Jody thought, of the mysterious box on the table in the den. What was it about that crazy thing that kept nagging at the back of his mind?

As T.J. set the table, he continued to glower at Jody.

"Don't be mad," Jody said. "*I'm* not. I was just telling you for your own good." He remembered, suddenly, all the times Dad had said that to *him*, and shuddered. Jody thought it was pretty creepy, giving advice to someone who—as a grown-up—had first told *him* the very same thing!

T.J. nodded glumly, as if perhaps he'd heard that speech before from his own father.

While Jody positioned the placemats and napkins, T.J. finished setting the table with silverware, crystal goblets, and pale blue china dishes. The familiar smell of sautéing onions sneaked under the door from the kitchen. It wouldn't be long, Jody thought. Mr. Anderson was due home from work any time now.

"What about some flowers?" Jody suggested. "Or maybe a candle?"

T.J., still contrite, found two stubby ones and some holders in a drawer, then went outside in search of flowers. Jody was deciding on a vase when Billy burst in, waving his menu masterpieces.

"All done! Look, Jody!"

Though Sally had obviously written the text, Billy had drawn an elaborate cake with sixteen candles on each card. At the top, *Shay* was crossed out, then *Chez Anderson* written below. "Wow! Good job!" Jody raised his hand in the air, and this time Billy met it, slapping palms as they'd finally learned to do in the cemetery.

"I like you for a brother," Billy said. "You're lots nicer than Teej."

Jody squirmed at the compliment. His cheeks went hot. "Let's put these on the table," he said, changing the subject. "That's the way."

He glanced up to see T.J. standing there, his fist full of tulips and daffodils. T.J.'s chin angled upward, defiant, leaving no doubt that he'd overheard Billy's comment.

"He didn't mean it," Jody said.

"Yes he did." T.J. scowled. "Hey, what do I care? He's just a little jerk."

Billy's lower lip wobbled and his eyes welled with tears. Jody slid an arm around his shoulders and glared at T.J. Why did he have to be that way? "Come on, Billy," Jody said. "Let's go see if we can help Sally." He pushed open the swinging door and let it flap closed between himself and T.J.

The kitchen tittered with the sound of vibrating pot lids and boiling water. Sally had put one of her mother's bib aprons on and was rushing between the cutting board and the stove, looking frazzled. Blond wisps had escaped her ponytail and hung about her face.

"What can *we* do?" Jody asked.

"Make the salads?"

"Okay." He'd never made one before, but how hard could it be?

"Great! You're a life saver! The stuff's in the sink."

Jody boosted Billy onto the counter, instructing him to tear the lettuce into little pieces while Jody hacked away at a fat carrot. His thoughts kept roaming back to T.J., still sulking, no doubt, in the other room. *He* was the jerk, not Billy. What was his problem, anyway?

"Jody's letting me help. See, Sally? Look!"

She turned and nodded, a silent "thanks" in her eyes.

From the living room came strains of classical music, first one piece then another, each ending abruptly. Apparently T.J. was following through without Jody on the rest of their job.

"Hey! Watch what you're doing!" Sally bellowed at him. "You're going to scratch the records!"

Records. Jody shook his head. It was hard to believe that cassette tapes and CDs hadn't yet been invented.

At last T.J. let one selection keep playing. Its grand sweeping tones seemed to suggest an unfolding story. Jody wondered whether it was from Mrs. Anderson's favorite ballet. Surely it would help set the mood for the dinner.

Soon the salad bowls were brimming. Jody put the fixings away in the refrigerator. "How are you doing with the meat?" he asked.

"Okay, I think. Does it smell all right? Maybe I used too much garlic."

"Smells good to me." Jody noticed the water in the pot of noodles foaming over. He tipped the lid as he'd seen his mother do.

"Hey, thanks." Sally smiled at him, then looked quickly away. "I wish Dad would get home. It's almost time to add the sour cream."

"Maybe you should just turn it off for a while," Jody said.

"You think?"

Jody shrugged. It couldn't hurt, could it? But then, what did he know about cooking?

"Okay, I'm turning it off," Sally announced, as if giving everyone one last chance to talk her out of it. "You guys better go put your waiter suits on. You know what to do?"

Billy plucked a dish towel from the counter and draped it over his arm. He pulled his face into such a serious expression that both Jody and Sally burst out laughing.

"What? What did I do?'"

Jody shook his head, unable to reply. It wasn't really that funny. Why couldn't he stop laughing? Why couldn't Sally? She was standing there by the stove, her legs crossed, tears running down her cheeks as she pointed at Billy.

A miniature waiter. Look at him! Taking his job so seriously. Jody howled at the thought, doubled over, hugged his sides. All at once, he began to cough. Sally slapped him on the back, her own laughter losing its grip.

Jody's spasm persisted.

"You okay?" She whacked him again—harder. "You want some water?"

Her concern touched him. Something deep within uncoiled, relaxed, and the cough subsided. He straightened again, taking care not to look at Billy, and gratefully accepted the glass Sally offered him.

While he drank, a draft stirred the steamy kitchen air. When Jody turned to look in the direction of the swinging door, T.J. blustered in like a sudden storm.

"Well, well, well." His dark gaze turned Jody's knees to rubber. "What do we have here? Looks like one brother too many, if you ask me."

Chapter 15

Something familiar flashed in T.J.'s eyes. Pain, maybe. Or at least what Jody had *thought* was pain back when Dad used-to-be-almost dying. But he could see now that there was more—a wounding, a closing down, a shutting out. Like when Jody and Mom would be talking, goofing around, and suddenly Dad would go off to his computer to work. Alone.

Sally broke the awkward silence. "One brother too many! *Honestly*, T.J.!"

"I'm not stupid, you know," T.J. said, turning back toward the dining room. "I see what's going on here. I can take a hint."

"Stop acting like a spoiled brat," Sally snapped, "and get in here before you ruin everything." When T.J. did not reply, she rolled her eyes and turned to Jody. "Can you go talk to him? Please?"

"Me? Won't that just make matters worse?"

"He'll get over it," Sally said.

"No, I'm serious," Jody persisted.

"Who knows, with him." Sally sighed. "Oh, never mind. Why bother? Let him waste his life being jealous. Why should we care?"

"You think T.J.'s jealous? Of *me*?" He reeled at the bizarre thought. Jody was no threat, and he certainly wasn't trying to turn Billy and Sally against their own brother. Why couldn't T.J. see that?

"I heard every word you said about me." T.J. swung the door wide. "It's like I told you last night, Jody—"

"At least *he's* helping," Sally interrupted, "which is more than I can say for you."

Cringing at her words, Jody jumped to T.J.'s defense. "He was doing the music, Sally. That, and the flowers."

T.J. twitched his lips from one side to the other. "This whole thing was my idea, you know," he said at last.

"Nobody said it wasn't," Sally repled wearily. "Now, would all of you please just stop this and go put your waiter suits on?"

Billy reached for Jody's hand, but Jody neatly avoided taking it and started for the den. Maybe T.J. was watching. Maybe he'd realize that Jody *wasn't* playing favorites. Billy seemed not to notice the slight and tagged after him.

"Don't be that way," Jody could hear Sally say to T.J. "He's *your* friend. You're the one who wanted him to stay."

Jody couldn't hear T.J.'s response from Mrs. Anderson's tiny den near the stairs, where they had laid out their uniforms: three white T-shirts, black string ties, and red plaid cummerbunds that Sally had cut from the skirt of an outgrown dress. Had Jody somehow worn out his welcome? Would T.J. send him away now? An ache lodged in his chest at the thought of such rejection by a *friend*, let alone by a kid who would someday be his own father.

Billy closed the door. With a sigh, Jody turned away. His gaze fell on the wooden box on the table. He eyed it longingly, wishing it would contain some magic balm to soothe bad feelings, to mend bitter hearts.

"You wanna hear it?" Billy asked.

"What?"

The boy pointed to where Jody had been looking. "I'm not 'posed to touch it, but if I'm real careful . . ." He lifted the lid and Jody bent closer to see a metal disk, a wind-up key, and some kind of mechanism inside. Billy touched a lever and the disk began to turn, sprinkling a delicate tune about the room like fairy dust.

Back and back Jody's mind raced, grasping at a time so distant as to be not quite even a memory. Scattered images filled his head. A smile. Crinkly eyes. Firm arms wrapped about him. And always the music, like stars spilling in an open window. Once, he realized now, there *had* been a moment of connection, of love, that went away—and came back—with these magical tinkling tones.

"Hey! Put that down. You're gonna break it." T.J. swept past Jody and wrenched the music box from Billy's hands. Clapping the lid shut, he glared at his brother.

"It's not *his* fault," Jody said. "I asked him to show me."

"Maybe so, but he knows better. You want Ma down here, all upset? Do you?"

Billy shook his head and began fumbling with his suit. T.J. replaced the music box and, ignoring Jody, started to put on his own outfit.

"T.J., lay off him," Jody said.

"Oh, like he's your brother now."

"You know, you're being a jerk, and you're going to wreck everything."

"I am not."

Jody sighed. "Look, there's no reason for you to be jealous. I'm not staying. I . . . I can't."

"That's what *you* think. All the others stayed, didn't they?"

"Yeah, but . . . I thought you wanted me here. Isn't that what you said?"

"I guess. But that was before I knew everybody was gonna like you better 'n me." He squinched up his face as if fighting sudden tears. "You were supposed to be *my* friend, not theirs."

"Why can't I be both?"

"Because . . . you just can't. That's all."

"But why?" Jody felt the heat rise in his cheeks. "Just because you say so?"

"Because somebody always feels left out, that's why," T.J. blurted. "Two's company, three's a crowd. Don't you know anything?"

Jody knew at once who *somebody* was. But it took a while to absorb the full impact of T.J.'s words. He tried to imagine them coming from his father, but could picture only that wounded look, followed by Dad's urgent need to hole up somewhere and write. "All I know," said Jody softly, "is I *am* your friend, T.J. That and a whole lot more. Honest."

Billy sidled up to T.J. then, asking for help with his tie and sash.

Relieved that the boy had had the good sense to ask his brother, Jody gazed out the door and into the living room at the broken TV. Still, T.J. said nothing, and Jody finally broke the silence. "Truce, okay?"

"All right, already. Sheesh!" T.J. rolled his eyes, but within moments his dimples surfaced, and Jody felt the knot in his stomach dissolve at last.

From the driveway came the growl of a car's engine, followed by the rumble-bang of the garage door.

"He's home! He's home!" Billy danced in place as if he had to go to the bathroom.

"Hold still," T.J. said. "Now I've got to tie it all over again."

"That's okay, Teej. You're a good tie-er."

Jody scrambled into his own waiter suit, grateful that Billy was playing up to T.J. After all the work they'd put into the anniversary dinner, there was no way Jody wanted T.J. to ruin it by sulking.

"Red alert! Red alert!" Sally yelled from the kitchen. "Everyone to their stations!"

As planned, T.J. went upstairs to get his mother. Billy took his post at the welcome desk they'd fashioned out of a TV tray. Jody hustled into the dining room to pour water and light the candles. He could hear Sally greeting Mr. Anderson at the back door: "Welcome to Chez Anderson, sir. Please meet your party in the front hall and wait to be seated."

"Smells mighty good in here." Tom Senior's shoes clacked across the floor.

"*Daddy!* No fair peeking."

Jody tossed a cloth napkin over his arm and stood at attention. So far, so good. Everything was going exactly as planned. Even his watch, sounding the countdown tone at 19:00, could not dampen his enthusiasm.

"Sir, do you have reservations?" Billy giggled.

"I think so," his father said.

"Ah—yes. Here . . . it . . . is." Billy read his lines in a halting voice. "Tomaso will . . . show you . . . to your . . . table."

Jody grinned. Tomaso. Nice touch. He wondered who had added it to the script. Sally, probably.

"Pssst!" T.J. hissed as he approached from the living room with his parents in tow. "The record!"

Jody blinked at Mrs. Anderson, unable to move. A fluffy pink dress swirled around her, airy and as light as cotton candy. Her shoulders were bare, except for the blond curls that brushed her skin. Jody didn't know much about ballerinas, but he supposed all she needed were satin slippers and she'd be ready to dance.

"Jodaso!" T.J. furrowed his brows and nodded sharply toward the record player.

Jody unglued his feet and fumbled with the strange machine. Cassettes and CDs were definitely easier to play. All you had to do was punch a button. But this! *Zzzzzrrrkkk.* Jody winced. He felt everyone's eyes upon him. "Sorry," he mumbled, and repositioned the arm at the beginning of the record—something called "Scheherazade" by a guy named Rimsky-Korsakov.

As the exotic music snaked throughout the room, T.J.'s mother smiled with recognition. Candlelight danced in her eyes. Jody rushed to pull her chair out and spread the napkin on her lap.

T.J. seated his father, then handed out the menus. "Our special tonight is Beef Stroganoff," he said.

Mr. Anderson looked as if he were having a hard time keeping a straight face. "Very good, Tomaso. We'll both have the special."

T.J. motioned Jody to follow him into the kitchen. The place was a mess. Pans and bowls and plates were strewn the length of the counter. Sally seemed close to tears.

"Just look at these!" She forked up a glob of noodles. They appeared to have turned to rubber.

"How'd you do that?" T.J. glared at her, and her lower lip wobbled dangerously.

"Don't worry about it," Jody said. "All you've got to do is put the sauce on top and it will be fine."

"Are you sure?"

"Absolutely," Jody lied.

"Okay, if you say so." Sally blew her bangs off her forehead. "Here goes nothing."

She spooned a sticky wad onto each plate and told Billy to mash it down. Then she ladled on the creamy meat sauce. "Don't forget the salads."

Jody hustled after T.J. with the bowls of lettuce that he and Billy had assembled earlier.

"Isn't this wonderful?" Mrs. Anderson turned from her husband to the boys. "You did this all by yourselves?"

Jody nodded. "It was T.J.'s idea. The whole thing."

T.J.'s earlobes pinkened right up at Jody's praise. "Everybody helped."

Jody held his breath as T.J.'s parents took their first bites. Their faces were frozen into enthusiastic masks.

"Mmmmm. Excellent," Mr. Anderson said. "My compliments to the chef."

"And mine." Mrs. Anderson nodded. "Very . . . tasty."

T.J. and Jody exchanged a worried look and headed for the kitchen.

"Well?" Sally said. "What did they say?"

"They said . . ." T.J.'s voice trailed off. His eyes darted away from Sally's. "You're not going to believe this, Sal. It's the best Beef Stroganoff they've ever tasted."

Jody unloosed a breath that he hadn't realized he'd been holding. Billy turned his right palm face up, waiting for Jody to slap it.

"You're kidding!" Sally's face could have lit a darkened room. "They really said that?"

"Yep," Jody said.

"How about the salad? Did they like the dressing?"

Dressing? T.J. looked as guilty as Jody felt.

"We . . . uh . . . we'll have to ask them," T.J. said, blocking Jody so Sally wouldn't see him fish the pink mayonnaise-and-catsup mixture out of the refrigerator.

Jody sneaked the bowl into the dining room and added a dollop to the Andersons' salads.

"Why, thank you, Jodaso." T.J.'s mother smiled. "May I have a little more?"

"Yes, ma'am." Drawing closer, he caught a whiff of her unusually sweet fragrance, something he imagined might come from exotic jungle flowers. Could this really be the same woman he'd visited so often in the nursing home? He stared in amazement, mechanically plopping more dressing on her salad.

"For criminy sakes!" Mr. Anderson said. "Will you look what you're doing?"

Jody recoiled in shame at the mess he'd made on her fancy place mat. How could he have totally missed her bowl?

"Flash, please. It was an accident." She turned to Jody. "Don't worry, dear. There's no real harm done."

"I-I'm so sorry," Jody stammered. "I'll go get a rag."

When he returned to the kitchen, Sally was pouring a jar of apricot jam into a pot while T.J. stirred with a wooden spoon. The floor was gritty with spilled sugar. Jody dampened a rag and hurried back to blot up the stain.

"It's okay, dear," Mrs. Anderson said. "Don't worry about it. Flash, tell him you're not upset."

Tom Senior's Adam's apple bobbed as he swallowed what he'd been chewing. "Claire's right, of course. Accidents happen."

Jody would have felt better if the man had actually apologized, but he guessed that was too much to hope for. Dad rarely apologized either, no matter how much Mom badgered him. Maybe it was a guy thing, or a family thing. Jody would have to remember to change that when *he* had kids.

"Yee-ouch!" someone shrieked from the kitchen. Sally, he thought. But it might have been T.J.

Mrs. Anderson started to get up, but Jody said, "No, no. You relax. I'll go check it out."

T.J.'s parents looked concerned.

"They're just making dessert," Jody explained. "What could go wrong?"

The smell of spent matches greeted him as he straight-armed the swinging door. Sally was running water over her finger. T.J. was fishing blackened bits of wood from the peach concoction on the stove.

"You all right?" Jody asked.

"She burned herself." Billy, seated on the drainboard, looked on, wide-eyed.

"It's nothing. Just red is all. See?" Sally offered her finger for his inspection. "The problem is the flambé. It won't flam—I mean, flame. Look at all the matches we tried. It's ruined."

"No it's not," T.J. said. "So what if it doesn't flame? Let's just pour it over the ice cream. It'll probably taste fine."

Jody peered at the sticky sauce. "You missed one," he said, pointing out an overlooked match.

"Whatever would I do without you?" Though T.J.'s voice held a sarcastic edge, his dimples deepened, and Jody realized that he was only teasing.

Even so, Jody sobered at the question. *What would I ever do without you?* Tomorrow, one way or another, T.J. would be able to answer it for himself. The thought hit Jody like a punch in the stomach. What if he wasn't able to time travel through the old TV before the repairman came? Then the child welfare worker would take him away for sure. Less than nineteen hours, that's all he had left. After that, it would probably be too late to get home at all.

Chapter 16

⊚ "That was great, wasn't it?' T.J.'s voice cut through the darkness.

Jody did not reply. All his attention, every nerve, felt riveted to the numbers that glowed 15:00. There was so little left of the 88:88 he'd begun his visit with. Surely there must be something he was meant to do. . . .

"You talking to me, Teej?" asked Billy, on the floor in another sleeping bag.

"Just talking," T.J. said, and sighed.

Jody rolled onto his side, plumping his pillow. Instead of dwelling on his own impending sense of doom, he focused on T.J.'s parents' faces, trying to burn the picture of their joy into his mind. "Yeah, it was great, all right," he said. "They even liked the peach stuff." He wrinkled his face up involuntarily, remembering the horrible taste. Maybe Sally had added too much brandy.

"I'll bet they liked it as much as going out to some fancy restaurant," T.J. said.

"More."

"Yeah, more," Billy chimed in.

"You really think so?"

"I know *my* parents would." Jody tried to push memories of them from his mind. It was easier that way, and besides, he *was* with Dad, kind of.

"How come you never talk about them?" T.J. asked. The very question set Jody's heart to pounding. "Don't you miss 'em?"

"Course he does, Teej. Every night he tries to go home but—"

"Don't tell me he's got *you* believing all that time-travel baloney." T.J. tossed off a scornful laugh.

Billy inched his sleeping bag closer to Jody's. "It's not nice to laugh," he said quietly. "How would *you* like to be lost in time?"

"I'm not lost, exactly. I mean, I'm with you guys, right?" Jody's own attempted laugh came out more like a grunt.

"Let's pretend for a minute you *are* from the future, okay? Then why aren't you dying to get back? All that modern, push-button stuff. Sixty channels on TV. Sheesh. I know I wouldn't stick around *here*."

"What's wrong with here?" Billy asked.

"Stop asking dumb questions," T.J. snapped, "or go sleep in your own room."

Jody patted Billy's bristly hair in the darkness, knowing T.J. wouldn't see and get all jealous again. Funny that T.J. should mention Jody's going back to watch television. He realized that he'd hardly even *thought* about TV lately. No doubt he'd set a record. If this continued, he's win that bet with his father, no sweat. That new bicycle was as good as his. But at the thought of the clunky old red one—the one T.J. had attached the "gas can" to—Jody's dislike softened with understanding. No wonder Dad had hesitated to junk it.

"I don't know about you, Jody Andrews," T.J. said. "I mean, really. Not one little thing. It's not fair. You know everything about me—what a jerk I can be and all."

"You're right about that." Jody grinned, but offered no sympathy.

"Well, you didn't have to agree with me," T.J. teased. "But, hey, you want to know the truth? I don't care *where* you came from. Really. So *don't* explain. It's no skin off *my* nose."

"Don't go getting mad now," Jody said. "It's better this way. Trust me, T.J. It's not safe to know too much."

"Safe for who?" T.J.'s question hung in the air. Jody shrank from answering it, afraid what he might say. "So be that way," T.J. declared at last, sounding more resigned than angry.

Guilt gnawed at Jody's insides. It wasn't just a friend he couldn't trust with the truth; it was his own father, the one person a kid should always be able to turn to. The thought rattled him all the more. But Billy snuggled into the crook of his arm then, bringing a strange sense of comfort.

"Well," T.J. said, and yawned, "I guess tomorrow's D–Day, huh?"

Jody supposed he meant Deadline Day for Mrs. Anderson to call child welfare. That sounded only slightly better than what he himself had been thinking—Disaster Day, what with 00:00 and whatever happened *then* rapidly approaching. "Yeah, it's D–Day, all right. When's that TV guy supposed to be here?"

T.J. murmured something, but it sounded as if he were drifting off to sleep.

"Mommy said right after lunch." Billy sought Jody's watch in the darkness and whispered, "It's still doing that countdown, right? After the TV gets fixed, then what's it gonna say?"

Subtracting quickly, Jody said, "Less than two hours, I think."

"Uh-oh."

"That's not much, is it?"

"Not unless you're gonna stay."

The boy sounded completely sincere, and Jody dared not scoff. He had to admit that having brothers and a sister around did have its good points. And it *was* kind of cool how one whistle could bring a whole bunch of kids running, eager to hang out and do crazy stuff like catch gophers and gas up their bicycles with water. If he went home, full-of-ideas T.J. would be *Dad*, off working all the time. Grandpa would be dead, and Jody would have to see Grandma again in the nursing home. The thought of her being crazy and alone, especially after having just seen her at the anniversary dinner, made the hairs on the back of his neck prickle. He'd never have to face any of that, if only he'd do as Billy suggested and stay.

But what about his parents? Could he even consider

disappearing forever from their lives?

"It's not so bad here, right?" Billy prodded.

"No," Jody said, "not bad at all." In truth—not that the boy would understand—it was rather like living in an old sitcom, only in color. Nice and safe—at least for the moment—in a way the future wasn't and never seemed to have been at all.

Billy curled closer. "Maybe Teej will play Spymaster with us tomorrow," he whispered. "We can try to demote him, okay?"

"Okay." Then, remembering Dad's boast about being the only kid who'd never been demoted from Spymaster, Jody grinned like that knowing TV-dial face. Somehow the thought of helping Billy defeat T.J. tomorrow—just once before Jody had to leave—filled him with a strange happiness.

In the morning, however, T.J. had other ideas. "It's nice outside," he said as they headed downstairs for breakfast. "Who wants to play in here?"

"Please, T.J.?" Jody realized that he was begging in that whiny voice he sometimes used with his father. Not good. But he only had 04:15 remaining on his watch. Every minute seemed precious and fleeting.

"It's 'portant. Come on, Teej," Billy chimed in as if he could somehow sense Jody's urgency. "Me and Jody tried to play, but we didn't do it right, did we, Jody?"

"Uh . . . no," Jody said. All at once he stopped in the front hall and stared at Billy, trying to make sense of what the kid had just said. Suddenly, a fire lit at the back of his brain. "It won't take long, T.J. Just one stupid game, that's all we want."

Billy agreed, his lips pressed tightly together as if to keep from blurting out something he shouldn't.

"We're riding bikes and that's final. You can be gas man," T.J. said to Jody.

"Who died and made you king?" Heat rose in Jody's cheeks. "I don't want to be gas man. What do you think about that?'

T.J.'s eyes narrowed. He looked like he was working up to saying something particularly nasty, when Mrs. Anderson came out of the kitchen.

"There you lazybones are! Come on in. Daddy's already gone to the market, but he'll see you at lunch unless Jody has to—" She broke off, pulled a worn tissue from her apron pocket, and dabbed at her nose. "You know I have to make that call this morning, don't you?"

Jody nodded, and she pressed on. "I don't want you to worry now, you hear? We've been through this before with other children. We'll get you back. You'll see." She walked him into the kitchen, and he could almost feel T.J.'s eyes hurling dagger-glances at his back. Jody still couldn't believe what he'd said to T.J.: *Who died and made you king?*

An uneasy truce hung like smog over the breakfast table, smothering any hope of conversation. Billy and T.J. took their seats and silently wolfed their mother's sausage and French toast. Though it was slathered with real butter and powdered sugar just the way Dad always made it, Jody struggled to choke down even a few pieces.

Why was T.J. being so bullheaded? Somehow, some way, Jody just had to get him to play Spymaster. Asking politely hadn't helped. Maybe T.J.'s father had never told him he was supposed to do whatever company wanted to do. Or, maybe, the problem was that T.J. did not consider Jody company.

What, he wondered, would TV good guys do when being nice didn't work? He couldn't exactly be mean to T.J. Still, there had to be another way. "Will you please excuse me?" he asked at last. "There's something I need to do."

"Of course, dear. I'll put your plate in the oven." Mrs. Anderson smiled, seemingly unruffled by his lack of explanation. He suspected that Mom would have needed more information before she'd have let him go. He couldn't help comparing Mrs. Anderson to those too-too perfect mothers on rerun TV, the ones his own mother was always complaining about. But maybe this was Mrs. Anderson's *company* self; when she was alone with Billy and T.J., maybe she was different.

"Hey," T.J. said around a huge bite of food. Powdered sugar spilled from one side of his mouth. "Where *are* you going?"

"I'll tell you later." Jody hurried upstairs to T.J.'s room, his heartbeat throbbing in his ears. His watch beeped at 04:00, spurring him on as he rummaged through the desk, not yet sure what he was looking for.

When he found T.J.'s leather marble bag, however, his stomach slammed up against his ribs. This has to work, he thought, dumping the contents into the drawer. It just *has* to.

Stuffing the bag in his pocket, he slipped out through the front door and stole around the house to the garage. The service door was unlocked, and there by T.J.'s bicycle was an extra can full of flattened bottle caps. With trembling fingers, he emptied it—along with others in the can on the back fender—into the marble bag. He cinched it closed. Then, with a backward glance toward the kitchen window, he took off at a jog in the direction of the golf course.

Chapter 17

Wet earth stained his hands, seeping under his nails in a way that chilled Jody straight to the bone. Even the smell, rich and musty, seemed to pierce his heart, bringing the sting of sudden tears to his eyes. Wherever he went, he would take this moment, this feeling, with him, even as he left something behind. Not many people could sink their hands deep and touch the roots of their past.

Head bent into the wind now, dirt hardening about his knuckles, he was nearing the Andersons' when Billy careened around the corner on his bicycle. His training wheels barely touched the ground. "Jody, come quick!" The boy's cheeks flushed crimson. "Somebody stole T.J.'s gas money! All of it!"

Jody jogged alongside, debating how much of the truth to tell the boy. "Don't worry, Billy. I know who took it."

"Really? Who?"

"Me. And I'm not gonna give it back till he plays Spymaster with us."

Billy's mouth hung open and his bicycle teetered

dangerously. Jody steadied the handlebars, steering him around a parked car. "T.J.'s gonna be really really mad at you."

"So what else is new? He's always mad at somebody, and I'm tired of it, aren't you?'

"Yes, but—"

"T.J. Anderson's not the only one who knows how to get what he wants." Jody raised his chin, defiant.

"But he's gonna get you, Jody. He gets everybody who messes with his stuff."

"Well, he won't get *me*."

"You hope," Billy said.

Jody raked his fingers through his hair in exasperation. "Look at this." He flashed his watch at Billy. Only three hours and fifteen minutes until zero-zero-zero-zero, whatever that meant. "See? What else could I *do*?"

The boy's eyes went wide. "We better hurry, Jody."

They started up Seneca Street. Someone was cycling in the middle of the road, his arms outstretched like a high-wire walker's. From the back, Jody couldn't tell who it was.

"What a showoff," Billy said. "What's so big about no hands?"

"Who is it?"

"Teej. But he's not s'posed to do that. Mommy tells him all the time, but he never listens."

"Let's catch up to him." Jody quickened his strides.

"Hey, Teej!" Billy yelled. "Wait for us!"

T.J. looked over his shoulder, and Jody closed the

distance between them. "And watch where you're going," Jody called, feeling suddenly more like a father than a son. "You don't have a helmet."

"A helmet? Ha! That's a good one. Look! No hands!"

An approaching red van caught Jody's eye. It loomed steadily closer, but T.J. seemed not to notice.

"Teej! Look out!" Jody lunged sideways in the same instant, knocking T.J. off the bicycle and into the gutter with a resounding grunt. The van screeched to a stop just inches from T.J.'s front tire. Jody struggled for breath as he rolled off T.J., the sky spinning overhead. He heard a car door slam. Moments later, a man in a red-striped uniform peered down at him, offering a hand.

"You all right, sonny?"

"I'm fine," Jody said. "But I don't know about my friend."

"Up you go." The driver pulled Jody to his feet, then bent over T.J. "How 'bout you, fellah? You all right?"

T.J. groaned but managed to sit up. A gash in his chin was bleeding all over his jacket. Just the sight of it made Jody reel. His reaction caught him off guard, and he staggered backward, fighting to regain his balance. The man produced a clean handkerchief and pressed it gently against T.J.'s face.

Billy. What had happened to him? Jody glanced about in a panic and realized that the boy had ditched his bicycle and taken a shortcut home through the neighbor's backyard. No doubt he would bring Mrs. Anderson running any minute.

"Oooh." T.J. winced and leaned back against the curb. "Is it gonna need stitches?"

"I don't know. Think you can stand?" The man eased an arm around T.J.'s shoulder and helped him up. "That was a crazy fool thing, not looking where you were going. Scared the liver right out of me."

"Sorry," T.J. mumbled.

Jody read the writing on the back of the man's shirt. *Dave's TV Repair*. The guy was early. *Hours* early. Sudden horror ripped at Jody's stomach. He had to get T.J. home, and fast. Had to patch him up and make him play Spymaster somehow. It was his last and only hope— unless he'd rather stay here with T.J., the know-it-all with his up-and-down moods. When Jody put it like that, he realized that his decision was easy. Living with Dad, overbusy but basically pleasant, won hands down.

"You should be thanking your lucky stars for this friend of yours," the man was saying. "Brave thing you did, son. Could have been hit yourself."

Jody squirmed at the compliment, which couldn't have been further from the truth. It hadn't taken bravery to throw T.J. from his bike; it had taken fear—sheer terror. If anything had happened to T.J. . . . . Jody couldn't even bear to imagine it. His watch beeped then—02:59 and still counting down. "Come on, Teej," he said, trying to iron the worry from his voice. "Let's get you home."

By this time, several women had come out of their houses and gathered nearby on the sidewalk. "Where's Claire?" one asked.

"Here she comes," another replied.

Mrs. Anderson raced toward them with a swiftness and grace that Jody could never have imagined. Matter of factly and without a word to anyone, she removed the cloth and checked T.J.'s chin. As he fought back tears, he seemed to be searching her face for a clue about how bad the cut was.

"He's real lucky, isn't he?" the man said. "Scared the liver right out of me, riding no hands, not even looking."

Mrs. Anderson nodded absently, apparently too concerned to even scold. "I think he's going to live," she said at last. "Thank God."

"Thank *Jody*, you mean." T.J. managed a half-smile. "He's the one pushed me clear of the truck."

"You did that?" Mrs. Anderson looked at him with that strange, searching gaze. It made him shiver, hide his dirt-caked hands like guilt in his pockets, and glance away. Could she somehow sense where he'd been, and why? "But of course you did," she said. "It's why God sent you, maybe."

"I-I don't know. I guess so," he mumbled, leaning over to retrieve T.J.'s bicycle as much as to escape whatever he might find in her eyes. He couldn't bear her thinking well of him, especially now, with his mind so full of himself and his escape plans. Besides, T.J. never would have even needed rescuing if Jody hadn't taken those bottle caps. . . .

Jody started off toward the Andersons' distinctive, red brick house, walking the bicycle. The handgrips felt strangely familiar and comforting, like favorite gloves. Behind him, he could hear T.J.'s mother still talking to the repairman, who said he had one other stop to make, plus his lunch break, before he'd arrive at their house. Instead of following Jody, T.J. clung to his mother, milking his injury for all the attention he could get.

Billy and Sally, waiting anxiously on the front lawn, rushed forward when Jody rounded the bend alone.

"Don't worry. He's all right," Jody announced. "Just a cut on his chin is all."

"That's good." Sally's pink-slicked lips turned up only slightly. She seemed to be debating whether to say something else. At last she blurted, "I can't believe I'm saying this—seeing as how you're *his* friend and all—but I'm actually going to be sorry to see you go."

"Go?" Jody's grasp tightened on the handlebars. Could she read his mind, or did she know something he didn't? "Go where? *When?*"

Billy sidled up beside him and checked the watch—02:40, now. Where were the minutes slipping away to?

"Mother says the child welfare lady's coming right after lunch," Sally said. "You've got to go to the home for a while."

The home. Jody cringed at the words. They reminded him of the place where Grandma lived in the future, away from her family, among strangers. If those welfare people got their hands on him, that's exactly how *he* would end up soon—and maybe forever. By the time they let him go back to the Andersons'—*if* they let him—their TV set would be as good as new.

"Pssst, Jody!" Billy motioned him closer, so he could whisper into his ear. "Can I tell Teej about the gas money?"

"Yeah. You do that. And tell him soon as his chin's fixed up, we've got to play. No stalling."

Billy darted off to deliver the message, while Jody put the bicycle away in the garage. His hand lingered on the two-tone seat. "Hope I see ya," he whispered to the shiny new Schwinn. A tickle started in his nose and he blinked quickly, fighting it off. At last, he went into the house.

His heartbeat seemed to pound out the minutes until Mrs. Anderson and T.J. finally came through the back door. Another lifetime passed before she had bandaged his chin and made him lie down in the living room.

"Too bad you can't watch TV," Sally said, not altogether smugly.

"It's getting fixed today, remember?" Billy said. "And I get to watch *Mickey Mouse Club*."

"Yes, but *he's* got to miss *Gunsmoke* for the rest of his life." With a toss of her ponytail, Sally headed for the stairs.

"*That's* the truth." T.J. sighed.

Don't worry, Jody thought. In thirty-something years you can watch all the reruns on cable.

"So *you* took my gas money, huh?" T.J. said at last. "What's the big deal with Spymaster? It's kind of a baby game if you ask me."

Jody and Billy exchanged a knowing look. Even if they told T.J. the real reason it was so important, he wouldn't believe them, Jody thought. And even if he did, could that knowledge somehow spoil things and keep the time travel from working? "I've never played before, that's why," Jody half-lied. "And Billy says there are all kinds of cool hiding places around here."

"What's the point? I know them all. I'd find you in a minute."

"So, fine. Humor me. Just one quick game."

"After lunch, okay? Maybe I'll feel better then."

"But—" Another beep at 01:59 made Jody's throat go suddenly dry.

"Dad'll be home any minute, right?" T.J. said.

Jody nodded dumbly. Lunch! That would take another hour! What if the repairman were early? Then what would he do? Still, T.J. looked so pitiful, lying there with that huge bandage on his chin. Jody couldn't exactly force him to play if he wasn't feeling up to it. "Okay," he said. "*Right* after lunch and no maybes."

"Okay. I promise."

"And no take-backs, either," Billy chimed in smugly, ready for any trick his brother might pull.

By the time Tom Senior arrived at twelve-fifteen, Jody felt as if a huge bomb were ticking inside his head. Only an hour-and-a-half until he was out of time. Playing News Flash only made things worse. He couldn't concentrate, and the egg-salad sandwich Mrs. Anderson had made felt like glue between his teeth. He could only manage a couple of bites.

"I'll put it in paper," T.J.'s mother said at last. "You'll take it with you—for later, for when you're hungry." Though she smiled encouragingly, there was a sadness in her eyes that made his own go suddenly hot.

Picking up the sandwich, Jody handed it over his shoulder to her without looking back. He felt the touch of her hands, then nothing. And he heard the hurry in her step as she hustled it over to the breadboard.

Too antsy to sit any longer, Jody stood up and shook down his jeans. T.J.'s father rose, too, and extended his hand—clean nails, carefully trimmed, Jody noticed. Unlike his own, still ragged and dirt-stained despite vigorous scrubbing.

"I've got to get back to the store," Mr. Anderson said. "But I meant what I said before. We'll do all we can to get you back here, and soon. You mark my words and take care of yourself, you hear?"

"Take care of *yourself*, too," Jody mumbled. He slipped his hand into the older man's and tried without success to return the firm grip. The words *ashes to ashes and dust to dust* echoed crazily in his mind. He pushed them away, wanting to memorize this moment exactly as it was and not taint it with the future. He wanted to look into the man's eyes and see his own reflected there, as Mrs. Anderson surely must have noticed. But all he could focus on was the pale half-moon of T.J.'s father's thumbnail. "Thank you, sir." His voice came out low and raspy, as if it were changing, as if *he* were changing by the man's mere handshake. "I mean . . . for everything."

Tom Senior nodded, and Mrs. Anderson waved them off. "You boys run along and play now—no roughhousing—or I'll have you all doing dishes, you hear?"

T.J. started up from the table. "Wanna play Monopoly?" he teased.

"You *know* what I want to play." Jody glanced back at the kitchen, marveling at how normal it seemed to see T.J.'s parents hugging each other good-bye.

Billy nudged his arm. "Whatsa time?" he hissed.

00:45. Jody turned the watch toward Billy.

"You're Spymaster, T.J., and me and Jody, we're gonna bring you down," the boy said. "So hardy-har-har!"

"No way, Billy. *You're* Spymaster."

"T.J.," Jody protested.

But T.J. only shrugged. "Fine. Then I'm not playing."

"Okay, okay," Billy said. "But then *you* are. Hurry up and lay out your calling cards." Before T.J. could even reply, Billy had covered his eyes and started counting, fast.

Jody made only a half-hearted attempt to hide, drawing the living room drapes about him. T.J., however, scrambled away in earnest. As Jody waited for Billy to find him, he stared at the fleeing minutes, his stomach pressing hard against his ribcage. By the time Billy flung back the fabric and tagged him, Jody's calling card in hand, the watch said 00:35.

"Come on, help me!" Billy said.

Together they scoured the house, from attic to basement. Upstairs, downstairs, then up and down once again. "Can't we give up?" Jody asked, his voice rising. "*Do* something, Billy. Make him come out! There's only ten minutes left!"

Billy nodded, then shouted up at the ceiling, "You are the master. You are the spy. Come into the light and look your servants in the eye!"

Jody took up the chant, racing upstairs, then down again, his legs buckling with fear. "T.J., I mean it. I'll never forgive you as long as I live if you don't come out here, right now!"

An electric mixer whirred in the kitchen. Jody shivered, dread growing at the sight of the broken television set.

"He'll come," Billy said, but in his eyes, Jody could read the boy's doubt.

00:08.

00:07.

00:06.

"T.J. Anderson," Jody started to threaten, but his voice cracked on the *son*.

"You rang?" With dimples blazing, the kid popped into the doorway as if someone had just shot him from an invisible cannon. He waved his captured calling card in triumph.

Relief swept through Jody, edging aside his anger. Still, he knew he had no time for either. "You're

Spymaster," he said, backing T.J. into the hall. "Now!"

"Hey. Don't you want to know where I was hiding? I'll show you."

"Later."

T.J. touched his bandage and winced as if Jody had just rewounded him. "Oh, all right, all right," T.J. said. "Lay out your calling cards and go hide already. Both of you."

Jody released the breath he'd been holding and grinned. 00:04.

"Do it, Jody," Billy urged. "Go on!"

"First give me high five."

The younger boy slapped palms without urging, then stepped aside, his eyes trained on his brother.

"What about you?" Jody asked.

"What about me?" T.J. smirked, then at last raised his hand; Jody met it halfway. The smack echoed in the foyer.

Jody's palm slid down T.J.'s, and paused just a heartbeat longer. A knot rose in his throat, making the words come hard. "Go hide your eyes, T.J., and count slow."

"One . . . two . . . three . . ."

Jody's gaze locked on the broken TV in the next room. Billy silently waved him toward it.

"Six . . . seven . . ."

Rooted there, Jody glanced about the room and finally at the younger boy, who kept nodding his encouragement.

"Go on," Billy whispered. "Hurry!"

The doorbell chimed a lilting tune. Jody stared hard at the front door as if he, like Superman, could see right through it. Who was there? The TV repairman? The child welfare lady?

His watch clicked from 00:02 to 00:01.

Either way, he was out of time.

With his pulse throbbing in his ears and his head reeling, Jody clasped Billy in a quick, awkward embrace. Then he dove for the broken television set.

"Teej, keep your eyes closed," he said, hurriedly folding himself inside. "No fair cheating now." But something nagged at the back of his brain, something he'd forgotten to do. Or say.

The doorbell rang once again. The mixer stopped. "I'll be right there," Mrs. Anderson sang out.

Then it came to him: *I forgot to tell where the bottle caps are!* In the same breath, his watch glowed 00:00, eerie purple in the sudden dark.

Chapter 18

The watch face faded until Jody could no longer see it, could no longer see anything—not even his own hands pressed tight in prayer. Damp fog swirled up, bathed in a vaguely familiar smell, musty and close as his own sweat. Through crackling static, a distant voice called, "Joooooooooo-deeeeeeeeee!"

Could he be coming *and* going in the same instant? Whose voice was reaching out to him like a lifeline in the dark?

Shakes wracked his body. He hugged them back to no avail. Maybe he was stuck, neither here nor there, like the object of some grand tug of war in time. Closing his eyes, he begged Billy and T.J. and Mrs. Anderson to let him go, and his own parents to call him home. A white roar filled his ears like ocean waves, relentless and powerful. At last a dim light shone through the fog, illuminating the opening in the old TV.

Jody caught his breath, letting his heartbeat slow as he inched forward and peered out. Grandma's worn furniture, camping gear, and stacked boxes—the familiar clutter of his own family's basement—greeted him like an embrace.

"Joooo-deeee! We give up, okaaaaay?" His father's voice wafted from somewhere above him. "You are the master. You are the spy. Come into the light and look your servants in the eye!"

Jody, suddenly confused, touched the inside of the hulk of a TV to ground himself. If this one had been repaired in the past, then why was it still just an empty shell now? His legs felt numb as he clambered out and steadied himself against the cabinet. Its weird dial-face grinned as if it still had all the answers, but wouldn't tell.

Jody realized that, despite his own frustration, he was grinning right back. He glanced at his watch, which now read SUN, APRIL 6, 9:28 PM. Calculating quickly, he realized that only eighty-eight minutes had elapsed since he'd climbed inside the old TV.

"Down here, Dad!" he called up at the ceiling. "In the basement!" He rubbed his legs, trying to ease some feeling back into them. At the thought of seeing his father again—seeing T.J. all grown up—his throat turned to cotton.

Dad's footsteps clumped down the stairs. "Well, *there* you are! I was beginning to think you'd disappeared into thin air!" He ruffled Jody's hair, and his touch, familiar yet not, made Jody's stomach rise and fall.

An image of T.J.'s pudgy, dimpled face superimposed itself over Dad's. Jody blinked both faces into focus, and T.J.'s gashed and bandaged chin disappeared beneath Dad's beard. "Me? Disappear in thin air? Now how could I do a thing like that?"

Jody held his breath, wondering whether his father would remember him from 1958. While that had been only minutes ago for Jody, a whole lifetime would have passed for Dad. But wouldn't he at least recall the explanation some strange kid had given about playing Spymaster in the old TV? Maybe not. Jody was likely to have been just one in a whole parade of foster children.

"Well." Dad folded his arms across his chest. "Guess I finally met my match, huh? Tell the truth now. Was that so bad?"

"Bad?" Jody gaped at him. "No, it was wonderful, amazing! The best thing ever!"

Dad inclined his head. "Uh-huh. Right. No need to be sarcastic."

"But I'm *not*. I mean it."

Dad laughed. "We *are* talking about Spymaster here, right? The *baby* game, isn't that what you called it?"

Jody swallowed hard, realizing his mistake at once. "Oh, sure. Spymaster. Best game in the world. Glad we played it." Again—*finally!*—even if I did have to bribe you.

Dad frowned, and, for a crazy moment, Jody feared that he might have spoken his thoughts aloud. With pounding heart, he watched his father stroke his beard and wondered, fleetingly, whether Dad wore it to hide a scar from that bicycle accident. At last his father shrugged and shook his head.

"What?" Jody's voice cracked. Had Dad remembered, after all?

"It's nothing. Never mind. Come on, let's go find your mom. She's upstairs tearing the closets apart, looking for you."

As they hit the first floor and started down the hall, the phone rang.

"Who'd be calling at this hour?" Dad muttered. "Not the paper, I hope." He answered on the second ring and passed the receiver to Jody.

The real question was, who would be calling *him*? For a strange disjointed moment, he almost expected it to be T.J. "Hello?"

"Jody, hey, it's me. Scott. Is your dad ragging you about me calling so late?"

"Uh . . . no." What could Scott Livesey be calling about—and, if Jody remembered correctly, long distance from his grandma's no less? "What's up?"

"You were supposed to let me know about the deal."

Jody turned away from his father in a half-hearted bid for some privacy. What deal? He couldn't begin to imagine what Scott was talking about. "I was?" Jody asked, his thoughts racing.

"You said you'd ask your dad, remember? And then you'd call and leave a message."

"Are you sure I didn't?"

"Not unless our machine's messed up or I did the remote code wrong. So? Tell me already. Name your price. Maybe I'll need some help from Grandma."

Jody rubbed his forehead. "Lay it out for me again, okay? I-I've had a lot on my mind."

"The Warren Spahn. Jeez, it's not like it's mint, you know. But I need it to complete my set. You said you'd ask if you could sell it."

"I . . . uh . . . haven't had a chance. Today's been kind of crazy. Easter and all. You'll be home tomorrow, right? Can I tell you then?"

Scott sighed. "I guess so. What's one more day?"

"Thanks," Jody said. "I'll call you."

"After eleven, okay?"

"Sure. No problem." Jody hung up and turned to Dad. He tried to form a question—about Scott, about the Warren Spahn card—but words refused him.

"Who was that?"

"Scott."

Dad accepted the news as if it were no great surprise. Jody frowned as he followed his father upstairs in search of Mom.

"Here he is, Ellen. Safe and sound, just like I told you," Dad called from the landing. In his eyes, Jody caught a glimpse of T.J., part braggart, part friend.

"Oh, thank goodness!" Mom rushed from Jody's room and met him in the hall. A blotchy rash spread from her cheeks to her neck, and a thin line of perspiration beaded her upper lip. "Where in the world *were* you?"

Before he could reply, she was smooshing his face against her T-shirt, hugging him close. His nose wrinkled involuntarily at the sharp musk that clung to her skin. What would she have been like, Jody wondered, if he'd actually been missing for *days*?

"He *says* he was in the basement." Dad shrugged. "Guess we must not have looked real well."

"Really? All that time?" Mom released him and touched his cheek affectionately. Her eyes sought his soul, and in that moment of connection, she seemed to spin a cocoon around them both.

"Well." Dad cleared his throat and moved away.

Refocusing his gaze beyond his mother, Jody saw the boy again in the man and understood. "Dad, wait!"

"No, that's okay." His father's face, so open and alive only moments before, slammed like a closed door between them. "I've got some work to do yet."

"Don't *be* like that," Jody blurted. "Aren't you even curious—"

"Your mom can fill me in."

"That's not the same, and you know it." Jody's lips twitched to one side.

At last Dad threw his hands up in surrender. "So, fine. I'm listening. How did we miss you?"

Jody debated how much truth he should tell. Just enough to see Dad's reaction. "I was inside Grandma's old TV."

Dad eyed him sharply. "Inside?"

Jody nodded, tried to sound matter-of-fact. "The picture tube's gone, you know, and I just kind of climbed in there and curled up."

"What a funny place to hide," Mom said.

Dad, however, did not reply. He was massaging the back of one hand with the other. His expression seemed far away.

"What's the matter?" Jody asked.

"Hmmmm?" His father blinked at him dumbly.

"I said, 'What's the matter?'"

"Nothing." Dad seemed to force a smile. "For a second there, you kind of reminded me of someone. Don't worry about it."

Jody bit the inside of his cheek, working up his courage. "How did the TV get broken, anyway?"

"Billy did it. He just kind of went crazy one day. I forget exactly why." Dad shook his head at the memory as if he still couldn't quite believe it. "Took the fire poker to the screen and smashed the living daylights out of it."

"Your brother? Are you kidding?" Jody's eyes went wide. How long after he left did that happen? "And you never ever got it fixed?"

"Nope." Dad didn't mention that once *he'd* broken it with his baseball and had to pay for the repair himself.

All those growing-up years with no TV, Jody thought. No wonder his father had such a thing about him watching it as much as he did. "Wow. That's amazing." Jody could hear the awe in his own voice.

"Poor Tom. Such a neglected child you were." Mom clucked her tongue, pretending sympathy. "And as for *you*, mister," she said to Jody, "time for bed." She followed him to his room, turned his covers down, then started toward the door. "You and Dad will have to manage dinner on your own tomorrow, okay? We're having a big after-Easter sale. I won't be home till late."

"Don't worry about us," Jody said. "We'll be fine."

Maybe better than fine. He could always hope.

"I thought so." Mom smiled. "Have a good sleep."

"No story tonight?" Immediately, Jody regretted asking the question and cringed. He expected his father to roll his eyes, to make some comment about Jody's being almost twelve. But Dad showed no reaction at all.

"Not tonight, sweetie. I've still got laundry to fold and—"

"It's okay. Maybe I'll reread *Charlotte's Web*." He stole a sideways glance at his father, hoping the book title might jog a memory. "Dad?" he prodded.

His father appeared to shake free of his thoughts. "Uh, sounds great, Joe. Good night."

"G'night."

Jody sighed as his parents' footfalls disappeared down the stairs. Closing the door, he glanced about his room. A familiar collection of sports caps dotted one wall. Mugsy poked her head out from under the bed and padded toward him.

"Hey, Mugs, how're you doing, huh? Did you miss me?" Jody scratched behind the calico cat's ears. Mugsy turned on her rattly purr. "Do you know anything about a Warren Spahn deal, huh, girl?"

Mugsy seemed to grin as if she, too, had answers but wouldn't tell. She reminded Jody of Grandma's strange TV. The similarity made him shiver. He checked around his room one more time, taking inventory. Everything seemed the same, precisely as he'd left it, and yet he had the weirdest feeling that something extraordinary was about to happen again. Drawing the shades, he changed out of his Brewers T-shirt and jeans and into a clean football jersey and sweatpants. Funny how T.J. and Billy always slept in baggy pajamas. Was Jody the only kid who preferred sleeping in regular clothes?

Mugsy leaped up on the desk then and pranced delicately over the neatly stacked books and sports magazines. As Jody reached for the cat, he started at the sight of *Stuesser's Price Guide* lying on top. What was that doing here? He wondered whether Scott might have slipped it into his backpack before vacation. But when he examined the thick magazine further, he noticed his own name on the inside cover.

"What in the world . . . ?" He leafed through the pages. There on page two hundred and five was a yellow highlighter pen slash over "1957 Warren Spahn, Near Mint." The price beside it read seventy-five dollars.

"But I don't collect baseball cards," he said, looking about his room as if it were haunted. "Do I?"

Mugsy brushed against the closet door. Jody sucked a steadying breath as he opened it and peered inside. Strange leather-bound binders he'd never seen before lined his shelves. He knelt and pulled one out, his heart beating fast. Sectioned plastic pages full of old Milwaukee Braves and other sports cards glared back at him. Eddie Mathews, Joe Adcock, Johnny Sain.

Hurrying now, he flipped through one volume after the other, in search of the '57 Warren Spahn. It had to be in one of them. But at last, Jody rocked back on his heels. A square, black metal door on the wall of his closet caught his eye. It looked like a safe or something.

Jody frowned. What would he need a thing like that for? Mugsy tilted her face toward Jody, regarding him as if he were the dumbest kid on earth. Of course, Jody thought. For cards! Good ones. *Old* ones.

He bit back a grin. So T.J. *had* taken his advice. What else could explain all this? With trading cards in common now, Jody supposed that he and Scott were probably better friends than he remembered. Weird, but definitely cool. He could hardly wait to find out what *else* was different in his life. And he would, starting tomorrow morning. After eleven.

Chapter 19

Jody clapped the receiver tight to his ear. "Scott? Hey, it's me, Jody. About that Warren Spahn"— he studied the card in question, wondering where Scott planned to get so much money—"how bad do you want it?"

"*Bad* bad. Why?"

"*Stuesser's* lists it at seventy-five dollars." How could he expect *anyone* to pay that much for a little piece of cardboard, let alone a guy who talked as if they were really—not maybe—best friends?

Scott gave a low whistle. "That much, huh?"

"That's what it says."

"Then that's what you'll get." Scott didn't even hesitate. "You want to come over? I finally found *End Around Football*, and it's not due till tonight."

"*End Around?* Really? That's great! I've been trying to find it for weeks at Video Max but it's always checked—" Jody interrupted himself in mid-thought, suddenly remembering his bet with his father. No TV, no video games. That was the deal. And by Jody's count, he still had thirteen days to go. Too bad he couldn't count the three days he'd gone without TV in the past. "Nah," he said slowly. "Maybe some other time."

"Right." Scott half-snorted, half-laughed. "Like you have something better to do."

"Maybe I do." Jody heard the mysterious tone in his own voice. "You want to come over and find out?'

A few hours later, when Jody burst into the house with Scott, the knees of their jeans were wet and muddy. Jody's cheeks, numb with cold, began to burn as the indoor warmth stole over them.

"Man, that was great!" Scott, blond and husky, collapsed on the floor. He was still breathing hard as he pulled his dirty sneakers off without untying them. "Did you see that gopher's eyes? He was like, 'Uh-oh. I think I took a wrong turn.' Man, I could have died laughing."

"You should have seen *your* eyes when he popped up in the jar."

"Yeah, well . . . how did I know it was really going to work? I thought you'd flipped out, Jode. Honest to God. I mean, what a crazy thing to do. But, hey, it was cool, wasn't it?" He babbled on like a play-by-play announcer reporting on a contest between Team Gopher and the Home Boys.

His enthusiasm swept Jody up, made his head spin. Scott *liked* it! Hadn't thought it was a dumb idea! Maybe they could do other things from the past together that wouldn't seem dumb either. . . .

Jody turned the thought over in his mind. There was no one around to play baseball with, and riding bikes was out of the question until he got his new one. Spymaster? Well, maybe. If they kept the basement off-limits. He wouldn't want Scott bumbling into the past, mucking things up.

"Hey, Jode, you got some cocoa or something? I'm freezing."

Jody led him into the kitchen, poured milk into two mugs, and slid them into the microwave. He remembered his slip of the tongue when talking to T.J., and suddenly wished he could have seen Dad's face the first time he ever nuked something.

"Stupid spring break," Scott muttered. "Can't count on the weather to be nice more 'n a day at a time, you know?"

Jody nodded. Only yesterday he'd worn a wind-breaker when they rode over to Grandma's. Now the sky, bleak and gray, held the promise of one last snowfall. Who could figure?

The microwave bell chimed and Jody removed the steaming mugs. As he stirred chocolate powder into each, he wondered what Grandma would think, in a few hours, when she looked out the window and found it snowing on the daffodils. No wonder she was confused. Who wouldn't be?

"Hey, man, what's with you?"

Jody shrugged. "I was just thinking. About my Grandma."

"The crazy one?"

"She's not crazy," Jody snapped.

"Hey"—Scott raised his hands and backed off—"those're your words, not mine."

"Well, I was wrong, okay?" Anger rose in Jody's cheeks, though he wasn't sure at whom it was directed. At himself? At Scott? At Grandma herself? "She's just . . . sick, that's all. Or maybe . . ." Jody's voice trailed off. Maybe she *wasn't*. Not anymore. Wasn't that just as possible as Dad collecting trading cards and Jody and Scott being best friends?

Scott raised one eyebrow and sipped at his cocoa. Jody stirred his, watching the steam curl upward and disappear. Sick or not, Grandma still had to be in there, someplace. Just as T.J. was still there, inside of Dad. If only Jody could reach them again. What he wouldn't give to have one more special time together like that anniversary dinner!

He glanced at his watch, noted the date. Two more days until his grandparents' big day—not that he expected Grandma to remember or celebrate it. Not without Grandpa. Still, Dad might think about it, might even remember making Beef Stroganoff and Peaches Flambé with some new foster kid.

And maybe—Jody grinned at the thought—he'd realize that that kid was really me.

The phone rang then, and Scott muttered a curse, slurped the rest of his hot chocolate, and scrambled to his feet. "How'd it get so late? It's probably my mom. Tell her I already left, okay?"

"Okay," Jody said. "See you."

By the time he answered, Scott was halfway down the street, his unzipped jacket flapping in the wind. To Jody's surprise, however, the caller was not Mrs. Livesey.

"Where have you been, anyway?" his father asked. "I was getting worried about you."

"Outside. With Scott." Jody decided not to mention the gopher. "He just left."

"Oh, well." In the background, Jody could hear the click of a keyboard. His father's, probably. "I was just calling to see what you want to do about dinner."

"Why don't we make something?" Jody blurted.

"Us? Are you kidding?" Dad laughed. "What did you have in mind? Peanut butter and brown sugar sandwiches?"

Jody smiled, remembering T.J.'s astonishment at the mention of the strange combination. "Oh, I don't know." He paused, hoping his suggestion might sound spontaneous. "How about Beef Stroganoff?"

"Beef . . . what? Give me a break, Joe. Let's just eat out, okay?"

Jody sighed. "Okay, fine. But I want to visit Grandma first. And you've go to be there, too."

"You want to visit Grandma?" Dad repeated, incredulous. "Two days in a row?"

"Yes," Jody said. "Can you meet me at five?"

"At Sunnyview? I-I guess so, but what's—"

"I'll explain everything then," Jody said. "Just promise you'll be there."

As he hung up the receiver, Jody glanced again at his watch. Whatever he was going to say to Grandma and Dad in less than two hours, it had better be good.

Chapter 20

Jody paused in the lobby, clutching the fistful of daffodils he'd rescued from the backyard. Maybe Grandma would like them. And even if she didn't, there was no sense leaving them outside to freeze. Squaring his shoulders, he headed toward her room. His pulse quickened.

In the main corridor, a throng of old people in wheelchairs blocked his way. Some pulled themselves along the handrails, their legs dangling, useless. Others maneuvered using only their feet. Many more just sat there, watching him too closely or staring off into space. As long as he didn't look deep into their eyes, he'd escape being sucked in, sucked under, by their sadness. Once I see Grandma again, he thought, I'll be all right. . . .

"Such a nice boy." A woman's papery-white hand reached out to touch him as he passed.

She was somebody's mother, he thought. Somebody's grandmother. He glanced back over his shoulder. Though her head shook with some kind of palsy, she greeted him with a toothy grin, then hunched her shoulders and waved like a kid.

Jody hesitated, then retraced his steps. He plucked a daffodil from the bunch and thrust it at her, suddenly shy. He could scarcely make his eyes meet hers. But it was okay; she was grinning so broadly that all he could see were two blue slits among a mess of wrinkles. Nothing more. No spark of real life or memory or anything.

He hurried on. Grandma's door was closed, but he could hear a muted male voice. Good. Dad was on time. Squirming with excitement, Jody spun the perfect scenario, imagining what he'd say to them both.

Somehow, he'd find just the right words to make Grandma's past come flooding back, and she'd call Dad "Tom" and Jody "Jody." She'd realize that her husband was dead and that she was living—and she'd come back to them. She would! And when Dad finally realized that Jody really *had* time traveled back to 1958—that they had actually been *friends*—everything would be different between them. Different, and better.

Eager now to set it all in motion, Jody knocked lightly. The male voice melted into some kind of classical music. Puzzled, he opened the door. Except for the radio, Grandma was alone. At the sight of her, he worked to bring into focus that long-ago dance teacher, a princess in her frothy pink gown. But the image refused to mesh with the frail, fuzzy-slippered woman in a wheelchair who sat there blinking at him now.

"You're late," she said. It was more an observation than a complaint.

But you didn't even know I was coming. Jody opened

his mouth, about to argue, but reconsidered. "I'm sorry. Here. I thought you might like these." He offered her the flowers.

"Well, I don't know." She gazed from the daffodils to Jody, bewildered, and her hands began to wash themselves in that peculiar way of hers. "I just don't know what to do with them, do you?"

"Maybe you have a vase," he said, and glanced about her room.

Grandma appeared to chew on that for a few moments. "I don't think so. But ask Tom. Yes, Tom will know."

"I will," Jody said. "He's supposed to be here any minute. He promised."

"Oh, he's a scallywag, that boy. Like I said to Flash, watch what he *does*. Don't listen to what he *says*."

"Really? You said that?" Jody pulled a chair up beside her, eager to hear more. Where *was* Dad, anyway? What could be keeping him?

Grandma's attention drifted away on a swell in the music. Her fingers, soft as milkweed fluff, seemed to float to her cheek. "Oh, my dear, this . . . this I *know*." She turned not to Jody, but to the empty chair where dad would have been sitting. Her eyes were full of questions, not answers.

"Maybe you danced to it," Jody suggested. He wished he knew more about ballet music.

"Flash, what is this?" she asked the empty chair. "I just can't recall."

Jody's stomach climbed and fell. She was talking to Grandpa as if he were sitting there—or as if his ghost were. Just the thought sent icy shivers down his spine. He fought to keep his voice steady, then ventured a guess. "Is it 'Scheherazade'?"

Grandma glanced about the room as if she were expecting somebody else to make a grand entrance. "No, no it's not, dear. It can't be. Not without Tomaso."

Jody's mouth went suddenly dry. "You remember . . . Tomaso?" he managed at last.

Grandma nodded. "And his precious little waiter suit, too."

Jody leaned closer. "What else?" he whispered. "What else do you remember?'

"Oh, everything." She smiled and her gaze traveled off to somewhere beyond Jody. "Every little thing about that night. Yes, indeed." Without prompting, she continued. "The invitation with the single rosebud. And the menu, of course. 'Our special tonight is Beef Stroganoff,' Tomaso says, and Flash replies—doing his best to keep a straight face, mind you—'Very good, Tomaso. We'll both have the special.'"

Jody listened in disbelief. His grandmother not only remembered the anniversary dinner, she kept spinning the story as if she were living it this very moment. "Tomaso's friend serves the salads, you see? And I turn to him and say, 'Why, thank you, Jodaso.'" Grandma paused, taking Jody's hands in hers. Someone's were trembling. He couldn't tell whose.

"You remember Jodaso, too?"

Her eyes met his in silent reply and held him captive. There was something there, somebody *home*. Then, seemingly out of the blue, she asked, "May I have a little more?"

The question caught him off balance. He'd lived this moment, these words. In the past, she'd wanted more salad dressing. But now, he froze, unsure what she expected of him.

"May I please have a little more?" she repeated.

At first, Jody's voice refused to work. But finally he eked out a "Yes, ma'am," and pretended to plop another spoonful onto an invisible salad bowl. He remembered how he'd missed—and how his grandfather had responded: "For criminy sakes, will you look what you're doing?"

"Flash, please." Grandma faced the empty chair again—the chair where Dad should have been, where maybe Grandpa's ghost was. "It was an accident."

At the sound of her voice, Jody's eyes went wide. Surely he'd only *remembered* Tom Senior's words, not spoken them aloud! Even so, his grandmother had actually replied, and now she turned back to him, touching her wrinkled hand to his cheek. "Don't worry, dear," she said. "There's no real harm done."

Jody blinked at her. His heartbeat drummed in his ears. He knew the next line, what he was supposed to say—what he *had* said—about being sorry and going to get a rag. But the words wouldn't come and his feet wouldn't move.

"Do you . . . do you know me?" He slipped from the chair and knelt beside his grandmother, searching her eyes for an answer. They were focused and full of light.

"Why, of course." She inclined her head slightly, pulled her hair over one shoulder, and began stroking it. "You're T.J.'s friend," she whispered. "Jody."

"Yes. I am."

"Andrews, isn't it?"

Jody's eyes went suddenly hot. "Not Andrews, Ander*son*. I'm T.J.'s *son*, Grandma. That's why you felt the connection, remember?"

"The connection?" Grandma looked from Jody to the empty chair, and back again. The light, he noticed, was fading, fading from her eyes. "T.J.'s son? I don't understand. I want to, but . . ." She smiled sadly.

Jody arose and kissed her cheek. He breathed in the soft powdery smell of her and closed his eyes to stop the burning. "It's all right, Grandma," he whispered. "I think maybe *I* understand. At least a little."

Absently, her fingers sought the hem of her housedress, and in not much more than a heartbeat, she was gone, disappearing into memories or time or a place only she could imagine.

"I-I'll be back," he mumbled, "as soon as I find Tomaso." Head ducked, rubbing his eyes with the back of his hand, he hurried from her room and down the hall. There was a phone in the lounge. He could call the newspaper. But no. Why bother? He was tired of Dad's excuses. And anyway, the TV was on full blast in there.

Jody paused outside, frustration building like storm clouds. The game show host's voice rose dramatically. He was announcing the fabulous prizes that today's champion would win. Just fifty more points, and this was the bonus round! The nursing-home residents, lined up now after supper in their wheelchairs, murmured appreciatively.

If Dad can break his promise, Jody thought, then so can I. Wiping his sweaty palms on his jeans, he inched along the wall toward the doorway. Soon the announcer's magnetic voice drowned out every last nagging thought. Of Grandma, of Dad—and the perfect moment he had totally missed.

Chapter 21

The announcer's voice continued to soothe Jody like salve on a skinned knee. Who needed to *watch* TV, when listening worked just fine? Squinching his eyes shut, he lingered in the doorway. But soon the familiar game show theme music lured him inside. He wondered what answers the contestants had written on their cards. What would it hurt to take one little peek? Dad wouldn't know.

The first thing he saw, however, was not the television, but the profile of an old man who gaped, slack-jawed, within arm's reach of the screen. His head was cocked to one side, and his left arm had fallen off a foam incline on his lap board. It hung, awkward and misshapen, like some outmoded tool he could neither use nor give away.

No one else seemed to notice. With frozen expressions, the other patients stared at the flashing images. They seemed plugged into the television as if it were some kind of life-support machine.

Jody crept forward, crouching low so he wouldn't block their view. His pulse raced as he reached for the old man's swollen arm and set it back onto the special armrest. "There. Is that better?"

The old man turned his head to meet Jody's gaze with one good eye. "Much. Thank you."

"Hush up, you two. We can't hear," one of the women snapped.

"Sorry," Jody mumbled.

The old man frowned as if he were trying to figure out who Jody was. Maybe one of his grandchildren. Did they ever visit? Jody wondered. What about his wife? What if she lived here, too, and they didn't even know each other anymore? Though the guy looked nothing like Grandpa Tom, Jody thought of his grandfather wistfully. Was his spirit really back there in the room with Grandma?

Grandma! Jody had forgotten all about her. "Look, I've got to go," he whispered to the old man. "I'll see you around, okay?" Without waiting for a reply, he hurried out of the lounge and back to her room.

"Teej?" Grandma frowned.

"No, it's me," Jody said. "I don't know where he is."

"He's a scallywag, you know. Always into something or other."

"Yes. You told me."

"I did? Maybe so." She smiled vaguely, but it was clear that he could have been anyone.

Some piano concerto was on the radio now. Grandma cocked her head, listening intently. Maybe the music was a link, Jody thought. A bridge to the past. Like that tinkly music box had been for *him*. With a sinking feeling, he glanced about the room. Surely he'd have noticed before now whether the wooden box were on display. What could have become of it?

"Flash," Grandma said, "do I know this?" She spoke to the air, it seemed, directly across from her.

Jody strained without success to detect even a shimmer or a ripple hanging there. He fidgeted with his hands.

"Yes, dear, I would like very much to dance with you," she whispered, extending her hand, but not to Jody. "Go on, take it."

Her tenderness and the memory of his grandfather ripped through Jody all at once like a hot knife through sherbet. Fighting back tears, he turned away and raced blindly down the hall. On his way out the front door, he bumped some man's shoulder, mumbled an apology, but didn't stop.

It was still light out, a glimmery dusk that bathed the western sky in blood. Budding trees and tall monuments in the cemetery across the way stood in sharp relief. Jody shuddered at the contrast, and yet he felt strangely drawn there, as if welcomed by an old friend. Was it really only yesterday that he'd been so spooked riding past it alone?

Without thinking, he crossed the street and jogged up the cemetery's main road, past the Civil War section where he and T.J.—he and Scott—had gone gophering. His feet crunched in the gravel as he turned down the lane toward the newer section that had once been a golf course. The great gnarled tree—noticeably thicker than he remembered it, and taller, too—loomed ahead like a beacon.

He slowed as he neared it, and let his breathing ease back to normal. Grandpa's smooth gray headstone sparkled in the fading light. Jody ran his hand along the cold surface. Was this really all that was left of his grandfather—a name and two dates carved in polished granite? All that would be left someday of Grandma and Dad and Jody himself? His mind railed against the images. Grandpa *did* live on, he thought. Inside each of them, inside everyone who loved and remembered him. And yet . . .

He remembered his father's words, his matter-of-fact tone: *Well, we're all dying, Jody. Hopefully, just not today.* Now he winced at the thought.

"Why, Grandpa?" he whispered. "Why does it have to be like this?" He listened, listened, deaf in the silence. Then he sank beside the tree, his back against the rough bark, squeezing his eyes shut to stop the sudden burning. But he was too late. Already tears were spilling onto his cheeks. Dampness seeped through his jeans, numbing the back of his thighs. Overhead in the empty branches, a squirrel chittered as if trying to console him.

After several moments, a shadowy chill, like the moon eclipsing the sun, crept over him. With a sniff, he opened his eyes. At the sight of his father, Jody scrambled to his feet, wiping his cheek with his jacket sleeve. "How long have *you* been standing there?"

"Long enough," Dad said. He was holding a package

the size of a shoebox. "Hey, don't sweat it about the bet, okay? You've been doing great. Everybody slips up now and then."

Jody frowned. "I don't know what you—"

"They told me you'd been in the TV lounge, and when you went tearing out of there the minute I arrived . . . well, I just thought . . ."

"It's nothing like that. Really. I didn't even watch TV." To his own amazement, he realized that he hadn't. "And I didn't see you, either. Honest."

"Well." Dad looked unconvinced. "Anyway, I'm sorry I'm so late. Did I miss anything? Is Grandma okay?"

Jody nodded, twitched his lips to one side. What was he supposed to say? It was over. Dad had missed *every-thing*, and there could be no reruns. "It doesn't matter," he said, and sighed. "I don't know why I thought it would in the first place."

"Hey, I said I'm sorry. I had to take an important call and then—"

"Why is everything more important than me?" Jody blurted.

"It's not and you know it."

"Knowing's not the same as feeling," Jody said quietly.

Dad blew out a long breath. "Look, I'm not Super-man. There's only so many hours in a day, you know? I'm doing the best I can."

"Maybe that's the problem. Too much *doing*. Why can't you just *be* sometimes, huh?"

"Because there's never enough time, can't you see

that?" Dad tugged at his beard in frustration. "What do you want me to do, Jody? Make more?"

"No. *Take* more. With me. Before . . . well—" Jody broke off, fumbling for the right words. "How do we know when it's going to be too late?"

Dad glanced at his father's headstone and nodded slowly. "You're right," he said at last. "We don't . . . we won't." His eyes searched Jody's, as if for an answer. But Jody had no idea what the question was. "So, I guess I'm too late, aren't I?"

"For some things," Jody said.

"But not for everything, right?" For an instant, Dad looked like T.J. had, that time he'd tried to get Jody to forgive him. Jody could almost see those dimples beneath Dad's beard. "Look. This came for you." He pushed the parcel at Jody like a peace offering. "I figured you'd *want* me to get it before the post office closed."

Jody blinked dumbly at the package. Who would be sending him something? What could it be? A crazy thought seized him. What if it were Grandma's music box?

"Go on. Open it."

Jody couldn't read the smudged return address. He ripped open the flaps. "What in the world?" He pulled out a hinged metal tin that resembled a pirate's chest. Inside, nestled in plastic Easter grass, were handfuls of chocolate candy coins.

"What's the matter? You were expecting something else, maybe?"

Jody hadn't realized that he must have looked disappointed. "Would you believe, Grandma's old music box?"

"You remember that thing? Lord, you were only a baby. Aunt Sally has it now."

"Really?" Jody's voice climbed an octave. He wasn't quite sure why he was so surprised, though. Aunt Sally *was* the oldest—and the only girl, too. Who else would Grandma give it to?

"Well?" Dad prodded. "Who's it from, Joe?"

"I-I don't know." Taped to the inside of the lid, he noticed a card monogrammed with WTA. He opened it and read the neat block-lettered message:

> *Happy Easter!*
> *Don't forget*
> *Your Uncle Bill*

Jody stared at it, speechless.

"Well, wasn't that nice of him."

Jody nodded, steadying himself against the tree. Dad didn't seem to find it unusual that Uncle Billy had sent him something. For all Jody remembered, his uncle could have been sending him things for years. Still, that he had received this particular package today set him reeling. He let the coins fall through his fingers absently, shaking his head.

"What's wrong? You still mad at me for being late? I thought you'd be *glad* I stopped for this."

"I-I am." Jody stammered. "But it reminds me of

204

something—something I almost forgot. A promise I made."

"What promise? No TV watching? Don't worry about it. I already told you—"

"No. It's not that." Jody's heartbeat thrummed in his ears. It had to be there. Had to work.

Setting the treasure chest down, he knelt beside the tree and located the root below the knothole, now barely visible for all the new bark growth. Like a dog in search of a bone, he tore into the wet earth with both hands. Root upon tangled root blocked his way. Surely no one else had found it. Panic rose in his chest. Try again!

"Hey, what on earth are you doing?"

"You'll see." I *hope.*

Clawing, frantic now, he opened a channel along the main root until he sensed a weakening, a space. Carefully, he eased his fingers into the cranny. They closed around something strange and squooshy, but about the right size. As he eased it from the earth, the covering all but gave way. Still, he cradled the unrecognizable lump in both hands, making his own peace offering to his father.

"What *is* that?"

Though Dad shrank at the sight of the muddy thing, Jody handed it over and said nothing. The familiar smell of earth, the feel of it beneath his fingernails again, made his stomach knot in anticipation.

Dad frowned, but dutifully poked at the end that seemed to have a string protruding from it. A faint metallic click came from inside. "What in tarnation . . . ?"

At Dad's words—*T.J.'s* words—excitement bubbled up like soda fizz inside Jody, but he held it back, giving away nothing.

Dad squeezed the lump, and something spilled from an opening. "It can't be . . . but . . . lookee here! This thing's chock full of smashed bottle caps. *Old* ones. Nehis, Bubble-Ups—just like we used to . . ." He shook his head and gaped at the odd assortment of soda-pop brands. "I haven't seen these for years. Bill said what's-his-name—this foster kid we once had—took them. Said he meant to give them back, only he ran away or something. Didn't want to go to the home, I guess. We looked all over, called the police, but . . ." He stared hard at Jody.

Time froze, or perhaps went spinning backward. Jody held his breath.

"Are you trying to tell me . . . ?" Dad's voice trailed off. "No way. It can't be."

"It was me, all right . . . T.J." Jody's huge grin stretched his face until his cheeks ached.

"But that's impossible." Dad kept shaking his head, like that wheelchair daffodil lady at Sunnyview. "I mean, Billy believed . . . right from the start. Always. But I never . . ."

"Well, if you ask me," Jody said, "nothing's impossible. Would you believe Grandma remembered me tonight?"

"She did? Really?"

Jody nodded. "She called me Jodaso, and for a minute there, she really knew me."

"Jodaso? Jo-da-so. . . ." Dad repeated the silly name slowly, and somehow, the way he said it, it sounded like a prayer. Suddenly he snapped his fingers. "From the dinner, right? The anniversary dinner!"

"*Now* do you believe?" Jody picked up the treasure chest and started toward his father.

"Well, maybe . . ." Dad hefted the disintegrating marble bag, then shrugged. "Maybe it's just a matter of time."

"Isn't *everything*?" The words, the very thought, seemed to come from somewhere outside Jody and pass through him like a shiver. He glanced about, but he and his father were alone.

Dad raised his hand then, and Jody met it halfway with his own dirty one. Their slapping palms pierced the stillness, and Jody grinned. T.J.'s old playfulness peeked out through Dad's eyes as he laced his stubby fingers in Jody's and squeezed tight.

Jody looked back at Grandpa's gravesite, at the tiny purple crocus that seemed to have appeared in a heartbeat. Then, cradling the treasure chest, he headed with Dad toward the unpaved lane.